To Barry and Helen

7/5/91.

Hugh F. Ryan.

On Borrowed Ground

"If you can look into the seeds of time
and say which grain will grow and which will not,
speak then to me . . . ."

Banquo
[*Macbeth*]

By the same author

The Kybe

Reprisal

The Kybe

'. . . a well-researched, well-constructed and well-told tale.' *Irish Times*

'. . . an attractive and well-told story with fresh dialogue and a strong Irish sense of place.' *Irish Press*

Reprisal

'. . . a human and humane account excellently told . . .' Kevin Myers, *Irish Times*

'. . . a finely written historical novel that is at ease with time and place . . .' *Sunday Press*

On Borrowed Ground

Hugh FitzGerald Ryan

WOLFHOUND PRESS

First published 1991 by
WOLFHOUND PRESS
68 Mountjoy Squarc,
Dublin 1.
© 1991 Hugh FitzGerald Ryan

All rights reserved. No part of this book may be reproduced or utilised in any form or by any means, electronic or mechanical, including photography, filming, recording or video recording, or by any information storage and retrieval system, or shall not by way of trade or otherwise be lent, resold, or otherwise circulated in any form of binding or cover other than that in which it is published, without prior permission in writing from the publisher. The moral rights of the author have been asserted.

Wolfhound Press receives financial assistance from The Arts Council/ An Chomhairle Ealaíon, Dublin, Ireland.

British Library Cataloguing in Publication Data

Ryan, Hugh FitzGerald
On borrowed ground
I. Title
823.914

ISBN 0-86327-295-9 PB
ISBN 0-86327-312-2 HB

This work is fiction. All characters, incidents and names have no connection with any persons living or dead. Any apparent resemblance is purely coincidental.

Cover illustration: 'Woman and Flowers',
a watercolour by Pauline Bewick,
from a private collection

Cover design by Jan de Fouw
Typesetting by Phototype-Set Ltd.
Printed in Ireland by Colour Books Ltd.

The beginning . . .

Imperceptibly at first, the ice rampart relaxed its hold on the land as the long winter relented. Weak and fitful, the sun took its toll with each warm season, fluting and fretting the face of the ice sheet, castellating its crest, while water trickled through its caverns and seeped from its base. The ice groaned, as if its spirit grieved within. It cringed as the sun, like a God reborn, hewed at its mass, and occasionally it advanced, with blizzards shrieking down the north wind, howling over the trackless wilderness of white.

But each year the sun returned with greater force, standing majestically in the sky, striking from on high, and the ice took on a new music as rivers flowed from it. The great mass divided as valleys drove into it. Like any army in disarray it abandoned its plunder, retreating to the higher ground. Water struggled with the crumbled rock, sorting and sifting, taking some and abandoning some, piling it here and tearing it away again, as it moulded a new landscape.

Deep within a toppling mountain of ice, in some luminous, echoing vortex, where waters met and laboured together, Brehonys' Hill was conceived. It emerged into the sunlight, a low, graceful parabola, standing unique and apart from the long diagonal scarp of boulder clay and above the morass where a stream had lost its way. Stabs of orange lichen appeared on stone. A seed, borne a long way on the upper air, drifted down and lodged in a crevice. The cry of geese sounded in the marsh. Like a new Genesis, the summers flowered and creeping things emerged on the face of the earth. Wolves prowled the hill. A great elk lifted his spread of antler on its summit. A bear grunted and stumbled through the young forest, pushing heedlessly through the tangle of briar. A boar rooted and snuffled in the deep leaf mould.

A straggle of pines gained a foothold on the skirt of the hill but the forest encroached no further. Tough, springy grass took hold between clumps of yellow furze where linnets whirred in springtime. But the geese came and went countless times and pine trees fell and mouldered, only to raise their gnarled limbs against the sky in a new generation, before voices echoed in the forest and smoke rose from the top of Brehonys' Hill.

One

I suppose you could say of the Sheehys and the Brehonys (usually pronounced Breeny in our part of the country, by the way), that their paths were inevitably entwined. Sheehys lived on the west side of the wood, looking down a long gentle slope towards the railway and the town beyond, while Brehonys lived beside the hill that bore their name, and they farmed the land around it, Brehonys' Bottoms.

My father always smiled at the name, as did we all. It conjured up an incongruous figure of Badger Brehony without his trousers, hilarious enough to the child's mind, but in later years I learned my father's deeper meaning, when I was old enough to take a drink with him and use the odd bit of profanity without a clip in the ear. He had a fair round of language himself, but only under dire provocation.

"Never," he used to say, "never devalue the four letter word," tapping my chest with a forefinger. "Don't devalue it, because there will be days when you will really need it."

He was right too. Nowadays it is in the mouths of infants and signifies nothing but a general disrespect for language.

His theory, based on a lifelong love of Hollywood, was that the film makers had to rely on code words which the more astute viewer learned to interpret.

Tom Mix never engaged in any overt sexual conduct "but," my father maintained, with a twinkle in his eye, "when he said to the girl, 'Some day I'm gonna git me some prime bottom land and raise me a herd of m'own', he was talking about screwing."

I was always slightly embarrassed by his use of the word, as if Tom Mix himself had uttered it. You rarely think of your parents in that way, as a rule, which is a bit of a contradiction.

Had I known of this theory years ago, it might have explained a bit about how things fell out.

Their paths, as I say, were entwined. Both families came across the fields to the town, their ways converging at a little timber bridge over the stream. They came through the railway station, the Sheehy children using the tunnel where they shrieked at the echoes. I can still hear their strong boots pounding on the flagstones. Their arrival was almost as exciting as the arrival of the train itself. There were only five of them, but by some trick they conveyed the impression of a crowd, a rout of red-haired little savages haring by on their way to school.

Badger Brehony crossed the tracks by the barrow-path at the signal box, a row of sleepers laid lengthways between the tracks. Even we were not allowed go across the barrow-path, although our father owned the station and had power of life and death over all. I always had a dread of catching my foot in the tracks anyway, and was glad of the prohibition. Sometimes on the old siding by the cinder heaps, I would put my foot into the rusting points just to satisfy myself that I could get it out again, but the fear remained nonetheless.

The children were wary of Badger, as he clumped along in his old gaberdine coat and rubber boots. He usually carried an ash plant tucked under one arm.

Kate, the eldest, was the only one who dared to speak to him. The boys gave him a wide berth, knowing full well that he knew who took his apples or set snares in his woods.

"Good morning, Mr Brehony," she would say, smiling brightly and tossing her long red hair. 'Titian' is the official term. Titian specialised in red-haired women and not a bad idea either.

"Aye, 'morra," Badger would grunt suspiciously, sometimes making a spasmodic jerk in the direction of his cap, not sure whether Kate was as yet entitled to the full deference due to womanhood. She gave the impression of a wisdom and experience beyond her years, which seemed to disconcert him.

We used to watch them at mass on a Sunday morning. We rarely went to mass in the town. It was much more pleasant to go up the hill to the little chapel where all the countryfolk went. The chapel was divided in two by a rail. The one-penny section at the back was tiled, whilst the threepenny section towards the altar was distinguished by floorboards. The gate in the rail swung across during mass and enclosed the last pew of the threepenny section, Brehonys' pew, as it had been since time began. Kate Sheehy took to arriving early, shepherding her brothers into Brehonys' pew and then closing the gate across while losing herself in her devotions. With eyes fixed on the crucifix and hands joined, she prayed and waited.

We nudged each other in delight when Badger and his mother arrived. She was an enormous, slow-moving woman with a perpetual respiratory problem. They would glare at the Sheehy children and mutter, but by this time the priest would have arrived.

"In nomine Patris et Filii et Spiritus Sancti." He always blessed himself with a whiplash action which stilled all coughing and shuffling. Badger would cast around for a space for his mother and occasionally we would stand up and offer ours. The three of us amounted to only one Mrs Brehony, but it was worth it. We Nugents were very well brought up as you can gather.

The priest twitched at the shoulder of his chasuble and glared around, irritated by the commotion. The Sheehy boys lowered their heads and looked at each other under their fringes.

"Introibo ad altare Dei." It was like a warning shot. Things settled down again while the saint at the end of the pew remained lost in prayer, her lips moving silently and her eyes fixed on The Crucified.

I sometimes wondered what Mrs Brehony went to mass for. She never seemed to like anyone. Maybe Brehonys had bought the pew in the beginning and had a right to it, but there was no name plate or anything like that on it. Kate Sheehy would do the same thing maybe three weeks in a row until she had Badger and his mother arriving a half an hour before mass, when old Miss Brien would only be opening the chapel. Then she might lay off for a month or two until Badger relaxed, secure in his possession. We knew what she was up to though, and sure enough the duel would start again.

I doubt if I said many prayers myself in those days, but I felt closer to God than I do now. I listened to the sonorous Latin, an age old mystery, and I watched the sun play on the plaster saints and the hair oil on the bowed heads in front of me. Sometimes the light caught in Kate Sheehy's hair where the headscarf failed to restrain it and the strands turned to fine-spun gold. Saint Paul rarely gets a good word nowadays, but I have to agree with him about women's hair. It was a wise move to cover it up in church. Look at all the trouble there has been since Vatican Two.

Old Mrs Brehony gave good value but Badger was a disappointment. He had the name of a hard man but all he ever did was sit in whatever seat he could find, occasionally flicking a glance at his adversary and wrinkling his forehead in a frown. From where I stood behind him I could see mud on his boots. In a childish way I thought of him as a poor earthbound creature.

My mother always sided with the Brehonys. She was some sort of a cousin and quite fond of Badger. "Little better than Tinkers," she snorted disparagingly. "Keep away from those Sheehys."

She never forgot the day that I went to school with Kate Sheehy. My older brothers were tired of dragging me along and had run on ahead. They had to be in for tables, they said, and could not wait. Kate Sheehy took me in tow. Strangely she was on her own that day. I was about six or seven at the time and easily impressed by older women. We went by a more circuitous route than usual. I remember squelching my toes in mud at the mill pond. We lay on the slab of stone that served as a footbridge and watched pinkeens in the shadow underneath, laughing at their expression of perpetual surprise.

There was a kestrel high in the sky over the mill, a rich hunting ground for mice and rats.

"That's a witch," said Kate staring upwards. The bird hung like a cross in the sky.

I shivered. The witch could, no doubt, see us clearly. We were at her mercy.

"It's my granny, so you needn't worry," she laughed seeing my expression. "All the Sheehys are witches and fairies."

"There's no such thing," I said stoutly. "That's only stories," but I kept a wary eye on the kestrel. Suddenly its wings buckled and it dropped like a meteor out of our sight behind the hill. I was glad when it was gone.

We shared our lunch and lay in the long grass. The milk had a taste from the newspaper stopper. It was a Powers naggin as I remember. She looked at my schoolbooks and said they were easy. I looked at hers. There were long stories with depressing black and white scraper-board pictures. I was glad I was not old.

I got into terrible trouble over that day, although it was generally agreed that it was Kate Sheehy's fault, but I remember it better than the many days on which I behaved in exemplary fashion. From this, I imagine, rose the general prohibition against associating with the Sheehys. Perhaps my mother divined in me at that early stage an inherent weakness of character, a fatal flaw which, if permitted, would set me on the path to ruin and depravity. Maybe she took the popular song about cigareets and whiskey and wild, wild women a bit too much to heart.

For a long time after that escapade I greeted Kate shyly but with a furtive smile to let her know we were still friends, until one day, passing with her brothers, she uttered the one word "snob", and I wanted to drown myself for an incoherent and spineless fool.

The injustice of it all! In daydreams I made her take back that word. She should see the fire that lurked below the surface. She would find that I was not a man to be lightly dismissed. I could take my father's bike and offer her a lift to school. At least I would do so as soon as I could get a leg over the crossbar. Time was on my side and, leaving out the problem of my mother, I would recapture the magic of that almost perfect day.

My father had more time for the Sheehys. Perhaps because his own life was ruled by timetables, signals and the whistle, he envied the less structured existence of Dan Sheehy and his unruly brood. Dan worked a few acres, kept a sagging glasshouse and a scrapyard overrun with hens and children. Weeds grew in profusion among raspberry canes. He never quite got around to wiring them up properly. Sometimes he left a dead animal in a field for weeks and trapped the foxes that came from miles around. Yellow buachallauns grew unmolested in his bits of fields and the 'noxious man' had given up trying to get him to cut them.

Squalor, my mother called it, while my father inclined towards a more bohemian interpretation. Although Dan was rough spoken and probably illiterate there was something of the poet in him, especially when it came to the internal combustion engine. In particular he loved motor bikes and allowed his yard to be used as the pits when the racing was revived after the War. There were almost tears in his eyes when he spoke of motor-bikes, especially of the Norton. The Norton, with the N stretching out to embrace the rest of the word, was the ultimate beauty that could be conceived by the mind of man. Not that he rode one himself, but he approached them with reverence and facilitated those who did ride them, as one privileged to serve a noble breed.

Locating the pits in Sheehy's yard during the race week gave the Sheehy children a status beyond that conferred by pedigree or money. They knew the riders by name and often got backers on the actual racing machines, while we, consumed with envy, were excluded from the inner sanctum and had to pay good money for Red X badges and autographs. Sometimes we managed to get in over the fence and stood around casually with hands in pockets, trying to look as much at home in the place as we could and scraping acquaintance with the Sheehys to give our trespass a gloss of legitimacy.

Dan Sheehy would take a gear-box apart with the assurance of a surgeon. We would watch in wonder as he laid the cogs and spindles out on a tarpaulin, like an exploded diagram, and then fit them all back again like a magician. Riders in tight leather suits squatted beside him in muttered consultation, or strode among the machines like knights at some slightly run-down provincial tournament, not Camelot and not quite Ashby de la Zouche, (I had read *Ivanhoe* by then), but one sufficiently important to attract some of the luminaries of the great jousts of arms.

Badger was assistant clerk of the course, an official of some standing, with an armband of commensurate importance. The Englishman's son was there too. He was, to me, like the first Plantagenet, an impoverished country knight in scuffed leathers and scratched pudding-bowl helmet. The Englishman as we thought of him, owned the land beyond Brehonys' and the decrepit old mansion that had seen better days. The planter, Badger called him, an English huer that stole the land off the Brehonys in Cromwell's time, bad cess to him.

He often bent my father's ear on his way through the station. He would gesture with his stick towards the line of trees on the skyline.

"That was all Brehony land at one time," he averred fiercely. "All Brehony land, till them huers came over." Three hundred years established no claim in his book. It was about time they all went back again. "Gentry, my arse!"

During race week, as a result of their common interests, Badger suspended hostilities with the Sheehys and he and Dan seemed to get on famously. He even smiled on Kate and her brothers and greeted the Englishman's son with a nod.

It was my job to bring the kettles of water over to the signal box. The station pump drew water from far down, freezing, crystal clear water without chemicals or little brown bugs, unlike the water from the taps.

There was always a fire in the signal box, even, I believe, during the War. My father and the signalman kept a kettle on the grate practically all the time in case of emergencies. This was their eyrie, from which they surveyed their world. Looking out from the end window I could see across the marsh to Brehonys' hill. In a tangle of twisted black trees the haunted house could be seen, sinister and gloomy like the stories surrounding it. A former Brehony had built it for grandeur, a solid stone house, worthy of any strong farmer, but it had been abandoned, or so the story went, because of the hideous sights that had been seen there and the midnight groans that chilled the blood. The stories were many, one better than another.

It had been built on an invisible fairy path and 'the gentry' had resented it. It had been built on a famine grave, on a stray sod, on a meeting of underground waters. It had been abandoned with all its furnishings intact and the table set for a meal. The very sight of it, even from that distance, filled us with delicious fear. The fact of the matter was that it had stood on the side of the hill for over a century, empty except for its ghosts.

A shotgun barked in the marsh, a sudden sharp report that came to us clearly on the wintry air, then echoed and re-echoed from the hill and from the woods. It was almost dusk.

"Badger at it again," remarked the signalman.

"Aye," nodded my father, warming his hands on his mug of tea. "A great man for the shooting."

"That he is," agreed the signalman.

I went to the door and stood outside on the step, leaning on the handrail. This had always been one of my favourite places. I could hear their desultory conversation and an occasional laugh. The signal box had always been a great place for stories.

My father told me there was a fairy fort on the hill. I could never be sure when he was being serious. He had lifted me up to see more clearly and told me that he had seen the fairies himself and the ghosts. I believed him at the time but, of course, I grew more sceptical as I got a bit older.

"I got such a fright that I jumped clean out of my skin."

"And what happened then?" I asked fearfully.

"Well when I looked around, somebody else was wearing it."

I knew of course, that he was exaggerating. "But did you really ever see fairies?"

"Well, no," he admitted, "They wouldn't come this far over. They like to stay near their hill. Anyway, they're afraid of the railway tracks." That seemed reasonable enough, seeing as how they were small people too.

"Fairies are afraid of iron, do you see?"

It seemed an odd explanation but it prompted in me a feeling that the signal box, being on that side of the tracks, was like a forward position, an observation post as it were, on the very fringe of the fairies' territory.

Sometimes people claimed that they saw lights dancing in the marsh but others scoffed and said that it was merely marsh gas, though who lit it I could not imagine. I did see a light moving on the hill one winter's evening. It was, I figured in retrospect, during the bad winter of 'forty seven. My father explained that it was Mr Brehony looking after his sheep.

If it was lambing time, that would suggest that the winter referred to was that of 'forty six/'forty seven but most people seem to remember 'forty seven/'forty eight as the bad winter. It may not matter very much now, as that winter has passed into folklore, but for tidiness' sake, I would like to be sure. I pride myself on a certain skill as a detective in such matters of little importance.

Nobody ever addressed Badger by his nickname, at least not to his face. He was always Mr Brehony to us or Ned to his contemporaries. Admittedly, when we thought it was safe, when he was maybe a quarter of a mile away walking along a headland, or just going out of sight behind a hedgerow, we might yell 'Badger' just to test for a reaction. Close up though, when we looked at the ash plant under his oxter, it was very definitely Mr Brehony.

Badger had been a fire-arms instructor with the L.D.F. during the war. He had held some rank in fact. My father and the signalman were reminiscing. I came in again out of the cold.

"All the same, you have to hand it to him. When the flying boats landed, wasn't it Badger that went out with the Civic Guards to arrest them?"

"True, true," nodded the signalman.

"And wasn't he the one that was ready to open fire on them?"

"A desperate man all right."

"People used to get up on his back about that. Dan Sheehy used to give him a fierce time over it. 'Ned,' says he one time, 'Why didn't ye put some class of a lashin' on them?' "

"Oh, he got very thick, right enough. He said they were invaders. 'In breach of our neutrality,' he used to say. He'd 've had us in the war," asserted the signalman, "and on the losin' side too." He chuckled at the humour of it all.

"Ah no, fair's fair now," my father protested. "I remember when he'd be out in all weathers at road-blocks, waiting for the Germans to land. There he'd be, with maybe his shotgun, stamping his feet all night and muttering."

"Aye," said the signalman, reaching again for the tea pot. "Remember what Dan says to him that time down at the railway bridge."

My father smiled in anticipation. The story was an old, familiar one that had taken on the patina of long handling.

"Dan scratches the head. You know the way he does it. He stands back and looks at the oul' sleeper on the pair o' blocks and walks around it. 'Begod Ned,' says he all serious like, 'isn't it a terrible pity the Belgians didn't have a couple o' them.' "

They both laughed together and I laughed too without being too sure why, but I was happy to be there in the warmth and companionship.

"Badger's reply was, as they say, unprintable," added my father, with a grin in my direction.

They sat for a long while in silence.

"In a way I suppose," mused my father, "he was as glad to be out in the elements, if you know what I mean."

"Aye," nodded the signalman ruefully, "she was a terrible woman. A regular tarmigan."

"A happy release, you might say."

"Aye, the poor woman," agreed the signalman solemnly, his face assuming the dolefulness obligatory when speaking of the departed.

My father laughed drily. "Not her, I mean. Poor Badger. It was a happy release for him."

"Hah!" laughed the other. "I take your point."

I looked for the word afterwards in a dictionary but could not find it. Badger had been married to a regular tarmigan. There was a game bird with a similar sounding name, but it began with a 'p'. Maybe Badger had shot them in his time but there was no suggestion that he had taken a gun to his wife. My detective work was getting me nowhere. Anyway the ptarmigan turns white in winter to render itself invisible. My mind wandered down another trail as they gossiped away in the warmth of their little retreat.

In the darkness I could see the parachutes drifting down, ghostly white, like owls, like thistledown, like snowflakes teeming out of the blackness to cover the land. I sensed the hulking presence of the enemy and I pictured Badger lying prone behind his sleeper, the shotgun at his shoulder as bullets whined under the railway arch. The name suited him. Dogged and tenacious, like his namesake, Badger defended his own. Tim Holt could not have done better. Tom Mix would have been proud to stand by his side, or more prudently, crouch by his side.

"You shouldn't laugh at him like that," I said suddenly, from the doorway. I felt myself blushing and suddenly ashamed, as if I had accused my father of something mean and low. "I mean." I gestured feebly, as if trying to take back the words.

My father looked momentarily surprised, then he stood up and ruffled my hair affectionately.

"Maybe you're right, Jamie lad," he conceded. "Maybe you're right. But sure, we meant no harm."

I forgave him, although there was nothing to forgive. It was I who had spoken out of turn, as I was only a child.

Two

My older brothers were mighty men on the sports field. They were away in boarding school, where they distinguished themselves, particularly at hurling. Fergal took pride in showing me his tongue, which had been bitten so often that it resembled a piece of tripe. Anto had his temple pushed in, whether intentionally or just in friendly high spirits I could never be sure, and lay in hospital in Cork for days while surgeons pulled the dinge back out again and fitted the jigsaw bone together. My parents went through a bad time then, but he made a complete recovery. He was no more or less mad after the experience and played with the same abandon as before.

There is an aspect of Irish Catholicism, much emphasised by the moral guardians of youth, that sees something meritorious in chasing a ball around a wet field on dismal winter afternoons, with a little gratuitous mayhem thrown in. I was never quite clear on the theology of this attitude, but suffered it in my time. It seemed a paradox though, that Father McBride spent many of his daylight hours running along the sideline exhorting schoolboys to 'pull on it, boy, pull on it' and much of the night seeing to it that they did no such thing.

There were advantages in my brothers being away in that I stood in the full blaze of my parents' benevolence, but there were disadvantages too. I missed their company on expeditions across the fields. I missed the occasional cigarette and the carrots we dug up to take the smell off our breath. I sometimes wished that my mother particularly, would take a little less interest in my goings and comings.

In the valley along by the sidings, which the railway builders had excavated to make the embankment across the marsh, we used to toboggan on old car mudguards. Some people improved the run by pouring frogspawn on the slope. This practice made me shiver in disgust. It was horrifying to think of all those lives crushed out to provide an afternoon's sport. Nevertheless it made a great slide and, since I was not responsible for spreading the stuff, it seemed all right to make use of it after the creatures were well and truly dead.

I often met the Sheehys there and since there was nobody else to play with, I invoked a kind of statute of limitations. The Sheehys had a good eye for a mudguard, I suppose, since they were in that line of business and we slid down the banks three and four to a toboggan with the running board rattling behind.

I know my father could see us from the signal box, but he never made any bones about the Sheehys and inevitably I got on good terms again with Kate.

She said that using frog spawn was disgusting and cruel and I agreed with her.

"Why do you do it then?" she challenged.

"I didn't do it," I replied self-righteously. "It was there when I came down. Some town lads must've put it there."

"That's just the same as doing it," she accused hotly.

"No it isn't. It wasn't my idea."

"That's what the Germans all said. They all said Hitler did it, when all the Jews were killed. They said it wasn't their idea."

"That's different," I protested. Of course it was different, but I knew very little about it anyway.

"No it isn't," she said loftily, "but maybe you'll understand when you're older."

"Huh," I retorted scathingly and lay back in the grass looking up at the sky. Somehow I had to regain her esteem.

"Do you want to see something that's really disgusting? I mean *really* disgusting." I had her attention. Her young brothers gathered round. She looked at me quizzically, even a little apprehensively.

"What?" she asked, raising an eyebrow.

"I'll show you," I said, jumping to my feet. "Come on." I ran through the long grass and up the incline towards the wagons on the siding, followed eagerly by the boys. Kate followed at a more sedate pace, looking sceptical.

"Axle grease," I declared triumphantly. "Look at this." I flipped open the lid of a box from which the grease oozed down on to the white metal bearing, and scooped a blob of the evil-smelling stuff onto my finger.

"Here, smell that," I said, poking it at one of the boys. He recoiled in horror.

"Phew!" he snorted, wrinkling his nose. "Now that *is* disgusting." I knew they would be impressed. In an instant we were chasing through the grass trying to smear the grease on each others' faces. Kate sniffed cursorily at the grease box.

"Boys are stupid," she announced to no one in particular and turned away, tossing her head in contempt. We looked at each other sheepishly and grinned. I stooped and wiped my hand clean on the grass.

"It is disgusting though, but," said one of the boys loyally.

"Yeah," agreed another. "It's the worst thing I ever smelled in my whole life. Worse than. . ."

"Yeah," the others nodded in vigorous agreement and I realised that I liked the Sheehys very much. They were men after my own heart.

The times of signal importance in our house were a half hour in the morning and again in the evening when the train crowds came and went to and from Dublin. I often watched them from my bedroom in the morning as they hurried along, almost always in the same sequence, two or three together, an individual or two, then another small group and so on, all united by the same anxiety. If one broke into a trot, the uncertainty spread and the whole crowd rippled with alarm. Elderly men lurched into higher gear, holding on to their pockets, and svelte young women tottered clumsily on high heels. The New Look was not built for speed.

Mr Devaney collapsed and died on one such occasion. He was quite a young man, they said, at forty-seven, which seemed to be stretching things to me. People talked about it for days and I wondered if he would ever be as important again.

The crowd gathered around, looking down at him. I could see white faces turning this way and that as they waited for help. People slowed and stopped in curiosity, and then detaching themselves from the group, they hurried on. I saw the priest kneeling beside him and the doctor opening his attaché case but it was all to no avail.

In school for weeks afterwards his son looked gaunt and haunted. He stood around in the yard with his hands in his pockets, staring at the ground and soon the family left the town altogether. I felt very sorry for him, but it was a relief when he was gone.

In the evening the same people debouched from the station, changed now by subtle alchemy. They chatted and smiled. This was oddly enough the time to avoid them. If you were coming head on, you were subjected to a series of greetings which had to be answered, a disconnected staccato of nods, helloes, names and smiles at the end of which you felt thoroughly foolish and the victim of some prank. Badger, on one occasion, it was said, after about a hundred yards of 'Joe, Tom, hello, evenin', nod,' lost his patience and concluding the litany with a 'kiss me arse' strode impassively on.

The radio was always on in our house and the morning crowd moved as often as not to Dvoràk's *Eighth Slavonic Dance*, suitably frantic for the occasion, or the B.B.C. Northern Ireland Light Orchestra's lilting *King of the Fairies*. The Home Service seemed to be limited in those days to two records and some incidental music, but it was preferable to the dreary hour of organ music followed by Victor Sylvester which cast a gloom over even the sunniest morning. I often wondered what hold the people of Kuala Lumpur had over poor Victor, that he was compelled to play exclusively for them. Never a dancing man myself, I pictured those sudden outbreaks of strict tempo at ten-thirty in the morning in that far flung outpost of empire. In later years I picked up his book in an idle moment, probably with a furtive desire to remedy my own incompetence, but there were no words. The people of Kuala Lumpur, half of whom have black feet, execute complicated geometrical movements with their white-footed partners, apparently without a word spoken. A strange and introverted race.

I loved the radio and spent hours trawling back and forth across the bands, watching the tuning eye flickering and winking as stations came and went. Dick Tracey and P.C. Bartley Willoughby, (Forty-Nine to you,) were high spots of the week, except when my mother was ironing. She had a lofty contempt for machinery and gadgetry, all of which she usually managed to break. The iron was attached to the socket by a knotted, contorted flex that occasionally smouldered and burst into flame. The socket wobbled on the wall as a result of her energetic movements. She could hardly be expected to worry about details. She had too much work to do. Did Nuvolari for that matter, pump up his own tyres?

My father eventually got around to fixing things in his own good time, but meanwhile, secret agents had to operate in a blare of static and interference.

In awe I say it, but I have seen her hoover up lighted cigarette butts and carry on complacently, with a blow-torch issuing from the other end of the device. She led without doubt, a charmed life. Our radio, I believe, exploded when the town went over to the new electricity. She had meant to switch it off to avoid the surge or something, but had forgotten. That of course was before my time, but it was down in the annals as yet another landmark in my mother's career of destruction.

Dan Sheehy had a windcharger that he had rigged himself. The mast and stays hummed and the vane twitched with every change in the wind's direction. The blades whirred in a blur. The boys said that their Da could see the world turning when he climbed to the top of the mast. I thought of the windcharger as a magical device, filching the strength of the wind and surrendering it to Dan Sheehy the wizard. Sheehy's radio did not get its music from the same tame domesticated source of power as the rest of us. It plucked it live from the ether and, when it crackled, you felt that it was the lightning speaking, just reminding you that it was around.

Kate loved Tom Jenkins most of all. It was not surprising that a girl would like that kind of thing but she had a passion for music. Apparently she sang around the house, but I never heard her. The nuns said that she had an exceptional voice and that it should be trained. Dan made no bones about a few bob for extra music classes, and Kate won medals at a feis, which pleased him mightily.

He had a wealth of old songs himself, old come-all-yes, which were very unfashionable in those days. Sometimes I stood quietly at the door of his shed and watched him. He sang as he worked, in a spray of blue sparks, welding or cutting a bit of metal. It was not that he had regular work but he liked to keep his hand in now and again.

"Sheehys was always metal-workers," he told me. "Tin smiths, copper smiths, that class o'thing. But now," he said proudly, "I'm erectin' steel."

"What's it going to be, Mr Sheehy?" I asked.

"That," says he, "is Badger Brehony's mast. I'm riggin' him a windcharger like me own and by God," he chuckled, "he'll pay through the nose for it too."

"Is he very rich?"

"Badger, is it? Sure he has pucks o'money." He picked up his torch again and lowered his visor.

"Stand back there now," he said and touched the rod to the metal. White hot liquid crawled and spat. He sang a snatch of a tune, which resounded strangely inside the visor and then stopped again. "Took us a while to get the hang of steel," he said meditatively.

"I don't suppose the fairies will be pleased if you put that up on the hill," I ventured, smiling and suddenly he was serious.

"Oh, good Christ, no. Ye couldn't put a thing like that on the hill. It'd most likely be blun down. I wouldn't chance it. No, this goes in the yard and he can take it or leave it."

The hill would have been the obvious place, but it went up in the yard with struts attached to the shed walls. Sometimes when the morning sun caught it I could see a glint of light just behind the haunted house and when I worked for Badger in the summer it was pleasant to lie in the grass at lunch time and watch the hypnotic motion of the blades flickering against the sky.

Three

When the laundry ink came out I knew that my days were numbered. The summer was at an end and I was to go to boarding school with my brothers. They had got thin strips of metal off fish boxes and had furbished their hurleys with a kind of keel and lengths of insulating tape. Everything was in order for them but I was washed and ironed and trimmed and admonished and told to make the most of my opportunity. I could not see why my mother would go through the travail of my birth only to cast me out, flesh of her flesh, to the tender mercies of what, on my brothers' say so, were certifiable lunatics and sadists, on the shoulder of a windy Munster mountain. Tears were shed and I saw more tears at Mallow, where small boys in short pants sat like refugees on their suitcases, while their older companions punched each other and shouted witticisms, renewing old acquaintance.

When somebody writes a symphony about that boarding school there will be an entire movement devoted to cabbage. Its spirit pervaded the place, seeping through corridors and into classrooms and coming between us and our prayers in chapel, a harbinger of culinary delights. It manifested itself three or four times a week, dark green and nourishing, full of iron, cooked with bread-soda to keep the colour, and totally inedible. It may well have been the same cabbage sent in year after year for I never saw anyone eat it. It was grown on the college farm and made good economic sense. To a sensitive soul like myself it symbolised my durance vile.

But there was another side to the coin. Father Rice, austere and fastidious, taught us History and Latin in the manner of one who had been there. Latin was his stock in trade, while his manner suggested that the great figures that loomed out of the darkness of history would have recognised in him a kindred spirit. Where de Mille reduced the epic to the banal or the absurd, Father Rice evoked it in his words. If Father Rice said such and such had happened, then that was what had happened. If Attila spared Rome at the request of the Pope, then undoubtedly a few bob had changed hands, because Father Rice said it would have been in character. Columbus got his ships, he suggested, with a faint glimmer of a smile, not because Ferdinand had an insatiable greed for conquest, but because he got to the king on a good day, the day in fact on which he had taken Granada and secured his place in history. To Ferdinand, he explained, this was the equivalent of winning the Munster Schools' hurling final, at which we grinned knowingly. We knew how his Catholic Majesty must have felt. On such a day anyone would indulge madmen and fools.

He had a terrible down on the early Christian saints and martyrs, which at first struck me as odd. In features he suggested a Torquemada, gaunt and ascetic, but the resemblance ended there. Decency and fair play were his guiding lights. I think he disliked the early Christians mainly for their strident inflexibility and the fact that they destroyed the classical world that he loved so much. In particular he disliked St. Simeon Stylites for his utter denial of life and the trouble he caused his poor mother. It was refreshing and also rather horrifying, to hear a priest speaking ill of saints of the church. Some other road to sanctity would have to be found for us, it seemed, as he threatened to kick our backsides if he ever heard of any of us carrying on like that. He would flick an invisible speck of chalk from the sleeve of his soutane.

The effect of Father Rice was a cumulative one, as he came with us from year to year, and in the end I came to think of his view of history as enlightened confusion, a compassionate absence of certainty. He sprang one on the class once, a scene sketched quickly on the blackboard, the settlers working the fields around the fort and redskins lurking in the forest.

"This is the scenario," he said with a wave of his hand and I thought of Hollywood. He must have read my thoughts. "Action," he continued, pointing at me. "What happens next?"

"Well," I began, frowning, "I suppose the Indians attack and kill a few people and then the others head for the fort. The cavalry probably gallop to the rescue."

"And the redskins bite the dust. Isn't that the way it should be?" We nodded dubiously, knowing there must be a catch.

"Right," he continued, "*Mutatis mutandis*. The redskins are now the O'Mores of Leix and Offaly and the fort is Maryborough. These settlers," he indicated the figures in the fields, bent over like so many commas, "are Queen Mary's loyal English planters. Now, where do you stand?"

Ah, that's different, I thought, feeling the shift in my head. I knew it was different because the Indians were painted savages, who scalped women and children.

"And Queen Mary was a Catholic, as you remember," he concluded, dusting off his diagram.

Not a real Catholic though, I thought. A real Catholic would never have done wrong to the Irish.

"And by the way," he went on like a conjuror producing another trick from his sleeve. "You remember how the Vandals cut down the fruit trees on their way through Spain."

"Yes, Father," we nodded. The Vandals had done quite a bit of damage, including the burning of the great library of Alexandria, which contained the bulk of Euclid's works, now irrevocably lost to the world and more particularly, to schoolboys. Muffled cheers, whenever this fact was adverted to.

"Well the Apaches never forgave Kit Carson for cutting down their peach trees."

I had seen Kit Carson. I could not imagine him doing anything so utterly mean and nasty. Incongruously, Badger came into my mind. A good boot in the arse was Badger's remedy for anyone who interfered with his apple trees. Carson (I was no longer on first name terms) thought he was pretty smart at laying traps, snaring his victims with a noose and a bent branch, but he would have his work cut out in Brehonys' woods.

Suddenly I could hear the ululations in the woods. The Sheehys, armed with bamboo bows and arrows, were attacking the settlers. I was blazing away from behind an old ash tree, my face pressed close to the elephant hide bark.

"More ammo, men," I roared as the twin Colts bucked in my hands. I could always hold them at bay until boredom set in, then we wandered off in search of some other adventure.

"Wake up, boy. You're daydreaming again." Father Rice ran a tight ship. I hoped that he could not see into my mind. Having driven off the red varmints, I was riding into the sunset with Kate Sheehy, with one manly arm around her waist. Her hair cascaded over her bare tanned shoulders as she turned her face up to mine.

I wondered momentarily about my saddle pommel and how she had accommodated herself to it, but only in a logistical sense. As yet my thoughts of Kate were pure, if wildly impractical. Perhaps it might have been better if she sat behind me with her arms around my waist. We could put off our moment of passion until we found some more comfortable position. Father Rice's intervention postponed the problem for the meantime.

"It might be profitable," he was saying, "now that James has rejoined us, to turn our attention to that silly ass, Rousseau, and his attitude to the noble redman."

I have never been able to think of Rousseau, ever since, as anything other than slightly dotty, with rather insanitary personal habits.

Mr O'Meara returned to school each year smelling of mothballs. He moved in an aura of camphor until about the first week of October. I wondered at first if he was hung in a wardrobe for the summer. He had come to the school long before the War and was as much a part of the institution as the school bell itself. He had married his landlady, a newsagent, in the village and, there being no issue from his loins, he had lost himself in his work. His suits, of an antique cut, glistened from long wear but no moth ever laid a tooth on them between June and September.

In summer he wore fawn linen jackets and pottered around his garden. I tried to imagine him as a young idealist coming to the village to spread the light of learning. I saw him in imagination, unpacking his fibre suitcase and placing his belongings in the chest of drawers. Landladies always line drawers with newspaper. Did he tilt his head sideways to read that the Bolsheviks had taken over in St. Petersburg or that Mr Logie Baird had patented a new device for sending pictures through the air? More likely he had sat glumly on his bed and reached for a notepad to let his family know that he had arrived safely and had a roof over his head. Gradually the camphor had entered into his soul and he had succumbed to the mothproof wiles of his landlady.

Mr O'Meara read books. He subscribed to *National Geographic, Life Magazine* and the *Saturday Evening Post*. He taught Geography and, from his own restricted world, he tried to open windows onto a wider world for his students. I suppose he got those magazines at the wholesale price, but he made them freely available to us in his classroom.

They spoke of an age of innocence, a Norman Rockwell world that seemed familiar to me, a world where people had time to stand around and chat. *Life* had colour photographs in an age when our everyday world seemed almost entirely monochrome. Shelves of *National Geographic* traced how mankind had evolved from a world of sepia to glorious colour. Kashmiris on the roof of the world held wonderfully coloured rugs out for my inspection. A Turkana woman collected sapphire dewdrops at sunrise, the first rays striking rainbows from each drop. A line of Mongol yurts straggled across the tawny immensity of the Gobi.

There were cartoons, slick American one-liners that taught as much about the land of the free as a library full of books: an old gentleman irately reprimanding a smiling television cowboy with, 'I'm not out in television-land, damn you! You're out in television-land.' I had seen television of course, in the window of a bicycle and radio shop at home. It seemed to be mainly about blizzards. I remember how the proprietor, intensely nationalistic as he was, had switched it off on the day of the coronation.

There was a cartoon which seemed to sum up in a backhanded way, the perennial dilemma of the settler: an old pioneer, reaching for the rifle over the fireplace, with the words, 'the horses is actin' up tonight, Maw,' while outside the cabin, a group of horses, like little gingerbread men, had obviously joined hooves to play ring-a-rosie. I thought it funny at the time and still do, but not everybody sees the joke.

But most of all *National Geographic* had breasts. We knew they existed in theory and had given them a fair amount of thought, but here they were in abundance and in every shape and size. It seemed as if everywhere else in the world, people lived in a state of primal innocence just because they were brown and black, while we, the superior race, were denied even a glimpse of the real thing. It was easy to see why we were of superior intelligence to the morons who passed for men in these articles. They seemed to be more interested in hacking out stupid canoes or spearing pigs, or filling baskets full of revolting looking yams, than in the wealth of mammary talent ranged around them. There he was with a bone through his nose or his lower lip distorted by a piece of oyster-shell, grinning at the camera and holding up some fish that he had managed to outwit, while all around him were young women, each with two breasts glistening in the sunshine.

A groan from behind would assure me that someone had come across *Bali, Jewel of the East Indies,* or *Safari Through Zululand.* Mr O'Meara broadened our horizons. The maps were very good too.

He used Eleanor Butler's books, because they had always been there, but demurred at the idea that Ireland is shaped like a saucer, being flat in the centre, "if you don't count the mountains in the middle and the fact that saucers are round," he would add. Likewise, he maintained, there was every probability that there were minerals in Ireland even though the book stated categorically that there were none.

"Do we look up the whole of Eleanor Butler for the exam, Sir?" was the standard question, as the term tests approached.

"Yes, yes, of course," he blinked over his glasses oblivious to the sniggers.

Yet when he talked about the landscape he became excited. A piece of limestone was part of a petrified sea. A piece of coal vibrated with the energy it contained. The rivers gave and the rivers took away and in his own way he blessed their infinite variety. He could often be seen standing staring at the tumble of clouds over the neighbouring mountains and he seemed to enjoy both fair and foul weather with equal enthusiasm. I felt that he was in touch with some great mystery which made him forget the mundane routine of his daily life. Of course we took it for granted that he was completely round the bend.

I wrote him an essay on the vegetation of the cinder heaps. I started it as a joke but, as it were, the subject grew on me. It intrigued me how, almost up to the point where the cinders still smouldered, the brambles twined along the ground. It was almost as if there were no roots. Their berries were poor, two or three pips at the most, but their relentless advance puzzled me. There was no soil to offer nourishment, yet everywhere rosettes of thistle and dandelion took root. Docks and nettles took up residence and also goldenrod and robin-run-the-hedge.

In summertime the thistledown and dandelion seed rose like a wraith of smoke.

"Excellent, young man," enthused Mr. O'Meara. "What you have described here in your own small way is the colonisation of new land, the very formation of soil."

He clenched the foolscap in his fist and shook it in approval, mangling the paper almost beyond redemption.

"But sir, why would things grow there at all, since there's no soil?"

"Aha," he said, "there you have it. Haven't you?" He shook a bony finger.

"What, sir?" I asked, not sure of what I had.

"The forest," he said urgently, leaning forward. "The forest reclaiming the land. It's still there, you know." He looked around. There seemed to be a wild glint in his eye. He smiled and relaxed. "Just a flight of fancy of my own," he said almost apologetically, "but I sometimes think the old primeval forest is still there, lurking in the hedgerows waiting for its opportunity to pounce."

We looked at each other half in amusement and he caught the sly conspiratorial looks. He rose from his perch on the edge of the table and paced around.

"All right," he said, tolerantly, "but just think of it like this. The parachute troops, the thistledown. Helicopters, the sycamores. Infantry-men creeping out across no-man's land, the brambles. Leave any field for a year or two and the perimeters close in. Give it a generation and the field is gone, I tell you."

I thought of Sheehys' fields, untended and unkempt. Mr O'Meara had a point. Something sinister lurked all around us.

"It's in every one of us too," he concluded ominously, "the savage, just below the surface." He stopped and stared out the window. We looked at each other and shrugged. Sometimes he would stare in silence at the hills for five or ten minutes, impervious to the shuffling and whispering behind his back, or to the flick of a paper bullet from a ruler.

"It's there still, all right," he mused and coughed. "Now let's get back to business."

Received opinion was obviously right about the bats in his belfry, but he made me think. I imagined that he made me think horizontally, where Father Rice made me think vertically. At the end of the year I did well in my tests and came home with a very complimentary report on my academic career, with the hope expressed that I would make a more concerted effort on the hurling field.

Four

Although my brothers arranged the jobs with Badger and, although he looked dubiously at me and suggested that I was a bit small, I was the one with the staying power. They only lasted a week while I stayed on and in a small way, made myself indispensable. In fairness, they were expected to handle hundredweight sacks while I was excused, but they were getting twelve and six a day to my eight bob.

Badger was a capricious taskmaster. Sometimes he would take a long lunch hour and go off in his old Volkswagen to back a horse, at which time we lay on the piles of sacks and smoked Woodbines, and another day he would work through until seven o'clock. We took to listening for the Angelus bell on these occasions and pausing in devotion until he dismissed the stratagem by saying:

"I wonder whose is the funeral," and started up the tractor again.

In time I had the run of the place. I brought in the cows and picked strawberries for the old woman. I collected eggs and fed pigs and generally made myself useful. I was very wary of old Mrs. Brehony. She distrusted strangers and watched me like a hawk when I was working around the yard.

For the first time I climbed to the top of the hill. The sheep had cropped the grass to a short springy sward between the furze bushes. On top of the hill was a tangle of stunted whitethorn and when I pushed my way through I found myself on the rim of a grassy bowl, the remains of the old ringfort.

The day was pleasant and I could not imagine why anyone could see anything sinister in the scene. So this was it, I thought, the fairy ring.

Maybe they would come and take me away and I would return in a day or two to find my parents long dead and my brothers turned into doddery old geezers. Serve them right too. I pictured them lying on the rocks at the bathing place, sunning themselves like seals and preening in front of the girls. They really fancied themselves.

I lay down on the spongy grass and prised off my boots. This was the life. I closed my eyes but the sun was still bright on my eyelids. I figured that Badger would be gone for a half an hour or so and the other spud pickers would be having their lunch.

I tried to cast my mind back over two thousand years to picture the people who might have lived there. The Fianna might well have sat there, roasting venison after the hunt. They ate a lot of venison in those days. I wondered what they did for spuds. A dinner is really only lunch without spuds. For thousands of years my ancestors had survived on lunches. They never even had tea because there was no tea. It must have been very peculiar.

A shadow passed over my eyelids and I started. I think I had almost fallen asleep. A figure stood between me and the sun, its head a blaze of light. I felt my heart give a jump with fright. The Banshee had come for me after all. I blinked into the glare.

"What are you doing here?" challenged Kate Sheehy. She moved towards me and I stared. Sprigs of gold surrounded her dark silhouette. I sat up guiltily.

"Nothing," I said causally, "just having a snooze."

I got the impression that she was annoyed with me and I felt like an intruder.

"Aren't you supposed to be working?" she demanded peremptorily.

"Naw," I drawled casually, "it's lunch hour. Anyway Badger has gone into town. He won't be back for a while."

She sat down a few feet from me and slipped off her sandals. She wiggled her toes and tucked one leg under her. Her dress was a light cotton check with no sleeves, and I noticed with interest that she definitely had breasts. I had never noticed that about her before. I watched her silently. She plucked a strand of grass and chewed it.

"It's warm, isn't it?" she remarked after a few minutes.

"Sure is," I agreed. "Anyway, what are you doing here?"

"Oh," she said, "I often come up here. It's nice and quiet."

My mind raced for something else to say. I wanted her to stay and talk to me.

"You gave me a fright," I admitted. "I thought you were a Banshee or something."

She laughed softly. "Do you believe in that kind of thing?"

"Well, not right now. I wouldn't be too sure at night though. What do you think?"

"Well, I'm not too sure about fairies but I think I believe in ghosts. Up here anyway."

"You told me once that all your family were fairies and witches."

She laughed again. "Did you believe me?"

"Naw," I laughed, "Though I wasn't too sure for a while."

"Would you go into the haunted house, then?" she asked, leaning over on her elbow. There was a pulse at the base of her throat. I watched it in fascination. Her skin was tanned except where the top two buttons of her dress were open. There was a definite glow of white skin there. My eyes flicked away as she looked up at me.

"I don't know," I said dubiously.

"If I was a witch, do you know what I would do?"

"No."

"I'd make strawberries grow on the bushes there."

"Strawberries!"

"Yes. I just love strawberries."

She turned over on her belly and tickled my chin with a long stem of grass. "Don't you like strawberries?"

I swallowed hard. Definitely there was more white skin visible. *National Geographic* was never like this. I leaped up.

"Stay there," I said and my voice squeaked. I coughed.

"I'll be back in a minute." I pulled on my boots and fled through the bushes and furze, oblivious of the thorns.

"What do you want?" snapped the old woman. She was sitting in the sun on a kitchen chair, like something out of J.M. Synge.

I looked around and spotted a pail.

"I have to get some water," I said quickly.

"Huh," she grunted, suspiciously, "well, you know where it is."

In seconds I was in the back garden and had stripped several strawberry plants without being too choosey. For good measure I threw in some goose-gobs and ran for the pump. By the time I had drawn the first splash of water up from the depths, the old woman's malevolent visage appeared at the back window of the cottage. I nodded and pumped away with a diligent frown.

I spilled most of the water on the way back but Kate seemed delighted with my loot.

"Hmm," she said, "not bad for a first try." She nibbled sensuously at a large juicy strawberry and I watched furtively. "Hmm! Have some yourself," she offered.

"Thanks," I said foolishly, without sarcasm.

"You're welcome."

"I can get more, any time you like," I said recklessly although, already, a little twinge of conscience stirred in my head. In a way I resented my own eagerness.

"Maybe," she said languidly, selecting a plump, ripe goose-berry. I heard her teeth puncture the skin and a soft sucking sound.

"Maybe," she said again, thoughtfully. "We'll see."

Suddenly I heard the bark of the tractor and I jumped up in alarm.

"I'd better get back," I said, almost relieved.

"Oh," she said and stretched luxuriously. "Come back tomorrow and bring some apples."

"Don't be daft. They're not even ripe. They're as hard as the hob." I snorted in derision.

"Just a couple," she said, putting her head to one side, "for me."

"That's stupid," I insisted, "you couldn't eat them."

"Don't bother then," she said airily. "It doesn't matter."

She dipped her hands into the pail and splashed some water over her face. The tractor rattled again.

"Ah, that's better," she gasped.

I watched a trickle of water run down her cheek, hang for a moment on her chin as if unsure of where to go and then, making a decision, it darted down the line of her throat and into her dress. My eyes followed it helplessly.

"Shouldn't you get back to work then?" she said again, almost dismissing me. In confusion I took the pail and swilled the water onto the grass.

"I'll be off then," I said awkwardly.

For some reason I was angry with myself, possibly because I had not cut a very masterful figure with her, or possibly because she made me feel like an intruder. In a way I felt she had been laughing at me.

The following day it was raining. I knew she would not turn up but I stole a couple of apples just in case. I stood around for a few minutes, well, maybe three quarters of an hour or so, just to be sure, and eventually I left the apples there for fear anyone might find them in my possession. I was glad that she was not there. It meant that I was independent, that I could go there by myself if I wanted to. In fact I decided to take my lunch up to the fort on fine days. I needed a bit of peace and quiet now and again.

When Badger was working, he went full tilt. First he turned out a couple of drills, then left the tractor on the headland and started to shake out. He worked back towards us and often met us half way. He had enormous hands and seemed to thresh the stalks as he came along. Shaking out was easier on the back than the actual picking because we were moving and throwing. He found it very amusing to pit himself against the younger lads, or maybe, on reflection, it was a means of getting more work out of us.

"When I was a lad," he would say, "there was no tractors. We had to get down and grovel for the spuds."

It seemed that we had life easy. I watched his hands. Three grazes on the knuckles and one thumbnail was black. 'The horny hands of peasants' came into my mind. That was a quote I think from that incredible lunkhead, Brutus, that Shakespeare wrote about. Gold, 'culled from the horny hands of peasants.' He would not have culled much gold from Badger. In the repetitive work of picking, a word would go round in my head. 'Culled, quelled, killed.'

Badger gathered potatoes, three or four in each hand and the baskets filled up. He was like a plunderer. Pillage, was the word. The ground yielded to him. They were good words, pillage, yield.

"Take a hand on that," he would say and I would help him with a basket. It was down a bit on my side. As we tipped the spuds into a sack he chatted while I gasped and tried to regain my breath.

"Are ye goin' to the motor bikes?"

"Oh yeah. Wouldn't miss it."

"Aye. Who do you think will win?"

I gave the matter some consideration.

"Hard to say," I said judiciously.

"Who's the best, then? Ernie Lyons?"

Ernie was almost everybody's hero because of his reckless style. Losing control of the bike was a matter of little importance to Ernie. He was in it for the fun and always seemed to survive by the skin of his teeth. Looking back after a skid or a wobble, he would grin in sheer good humour at the whole business. Ernie was indestructible.

"Naw," I replied, "but he's pretty good though."

"What about the Carters?"

If I could keep him talking, he might slow down a bit, maybe even stop for a smoke.

"Not bad either." By virtue of Father Rice's tutelage, I had come to see them as the two thunderbolts of war. Thunder was the word for them, especially under the railway bridge, exhausts bellowing as they blasted into the corner.

"Your man up the road is good too," I ventured, "Olford." It was as if a shadow passed over the sun. Badger scowled and spat.

"J.W. Olford," he sneered, "not worth a damn."

He gathered the top of the sack and stitched across with an enormous, curved sacking needle, pulling the twine with the heel of his hand and forming an ear at each corner. The twine bit into his hand as he twisted and pulled.

"The Englishman," he said abstractedly. "Not worth a damn."

He stabbed the needle into the ball of twine.

"Well, young fella, we can't stand around chattin' all day. There's work to be done."

He was off again, bending and gathering and the rest of us trying to keep pace with him.

I had not mentioned number sixty-three, Manliffe Barrington. In the railway bridge the other bikes bayed his name. 'Barrington, Barrington', as if in despair, for they knew that he was gaining on them, relentlessly clawing back his handicap with each lap. Crouched low over the tank of his Norton, he was the predator. He struck fear and despair into the hearts of lesser men. They scattered like sheep before the wolf and defeat was a palpable thing. In desperation they flattened themselves and wrung their throttles, but when Barrington passed through the bunch they sat appreciably more upright, almost relieved at being able to give up.

He was the Launcelot of my world but his name was not lightly spoken. There was no need to compare him with others. Barrington was the lightning. *Fulmen*, *fulminis*, neuter, the lightning. I reached for the spuds, grovelling in the clay. A horsefly, trailing an undercarriage, landed on my arm and eyed me insolently. I watched it for a moment in indecision. It appeared to hitch itself up and suddenly it stung into the skin.

"Ouch," I yelled and slapped it into a brown smear. "The bastard."

Badger laughed as I rubbed at the swelling.

"Always get him before he gets you," he chuckled.

Five

On the day of the races he let us off early and life was good as I jingled forty-five bob in my trousers pocket.

"Here," he said benignly, infected by the holiday atmosphere, "take a couple of punnets and bring some strawberries home to the mammy."

I wasted no time and dashed around to the garden. I could feel the old woman's eyes on me from behind the lace curtain.

Badger had shot a couple of jackdaws and had strung them on the raspberry wires, complaining that they were eating him out of house and home. They dangled in the breeze, their lifeless wings spread out and hooded, grey heads lolling. I imagined that they also were watching me. The strawberries were coming to an end but the raspberries had to be protected too. Offhand I wondered if they had died for my theft but reasoned that they were incorrigible thieves anyway.

Anticipation was the best part; the tar bubbling on the road; the crowds pouring from the trains and jostling for a vantage point on walls and ditches; the hawkers with their trays of chocolate and oranges. It was essential to be there early on the railway bank. A minute's delay could mean that someone else got the perfect position and you might have to go higher where there were ants, or lower where part of the approach road was obscured by hedges.

The trains nudged apologetically through the crowds and people cheered and waved for no good reason. The marshals were cheered derisively as they purred past on their final inspection and then at last the official car announced that the road was closed.

A hush descended as people strained for the first sounds. Programmes were checked and pencils held at the ready.

Thin and far away there rose a wavering whine. The smaller bikes had started and had gone into the country. A deeper note followed as the pursuit revved up and finally the deep bass of the five hundreds rumbled on the wind as the great machines thundered their manifestoes.

A flash of white between the distant hedges and the first rider was in sight, going hell for leather. He was duly ticked off, the leader, if only for a lap. Then came a procession of venerable machines, *Excelsior, Matchless, Velocette, Ariel,* some of them pre-war with rigid front forks and an almost Edwardian dignity about them. They roared and barked as they entered the bridge and the smell of high octane pervaded the air, but they fooled nobody.

Their demeanour betrayed them and we knew that the dogs of war had been let loose. These were no ordinary men. Lyons, Carter, McCandless, Olford, Carter and finally Barrington. We shouted their names like a litany, an incantation over the crescendo of noise and pointed excitedly, explaining the finer points to one another. Everything after them was anti-climax.

The minnows fled by, possibly with even the winner among them, but we waited for the real race and there they were again, a glittering constellation hurtling through space, the sun glancing from spokes and helmets. Lyons, Carter, Olford, Barrington, McCandless and Carter. Partisan arguments broke out and threats were made. We ran across the tracks to watch them speeding down into the town, every gear change a howl of defiance.

"Barrington has him."

"No, he hasn't."

I should have wanted the local man to win, but my first loyalty was to Barrington.

We strained our ears again. Anything could happen in seven miles. A marshal puttered obsequiously along and drew in to the side to let a cluster of riders pass. We wondered how a man could sink so low.

Dot, A.J.S., a bilious red *Moto Guzzi*, a name that excited laughter and there they were again, the wolfpack, Olford, Barrington, Carter, McCandless.

"Where's Lyons?" The second Carter limped into sight, black smoke billowing behind him. Dejectedly he poled his machine into the lay-by and dismounted.

"Lyons . . .' The name rippled through the crowd.

"What happened to Lyons?" and then we saw him, perched on the marshal's pillion, with his helmet slung over his elbow. A trifling matter of a demolished gate-pillar and a dismantled machine apparently. He grinned like a schoolboy and leaned over to share a joke with the marshal.

"Mad bastard," said someone in admiration. There was no more to be said. It was Barrington, Olford, Carter, McCandless from then on, with variations on second, third and fourth positions, but Barrington had set his stamp on the race, with a new lap record. Some experts maintained that Olford could have taken him again if he had been on a Norton, but Olford was a dedicated B.S.A. man, having graduated from his first ancient machine, and could hardly be expected to change allegiance just for vainglory. Why a man though, would choose not to ride a *Norton* was a mystery. It suggested a certain weakness of mind, but he had done well nonetheless.

"I will go unto the altar of God."

The priest intoned in Latin and I followed his words in the missal. It was my mother's missal in fact, with limp coloured ribbons hanging out of it and memorial cards tucked here and there. It had a hand-tooled leather cover and I thought it a pretty impressive piece of work.

"To God, who gives joy to my youth," I read. The priest was hardly a youth, with his few grey ribs of hair carefully plastered across his bald patch. In those days they got on with their business without the matiness of the vernacular, with their backs to the congregation and none of the awkward mummery of responses and hand-shaking. I wondered if he ever checked with a second mirror to see the effect from the back. He should have.

The Brehonys were in their proper pew and the Sheehy children were ranged in the front seat, using the communion rail as their kneeler. God was in His heaven and although the motor-bikes had departed for another year, all was right with the world, except for the odd broken fence and a bit of trampled barley. The work of the city people who knew no better anyway.

I could never find the Proper of the day or the correct readings, so I contented myself with looking around and occasionally ruffling the pages with a devotional air.

"To God Who gives joy to my youth." He wasn't doing a bad job of it, I had to admit.

I went to the pictures with my father. My mother would never go on a Sunday. The film was *The African Queen*, about an old couple coming downriver in a ramshackle boat, for some reason. It was all a bit confusing in that many of the German soldiers were black, but immediately I recognised Badger in the hero. He was about the same age and was just as scruffy looking. I put the theory to my father who laughed.

"You know, you're right. I never thought of Badger as a film star."

Bogart had much the same approach to machinery as Badger, using a spanner for most jobs especially hammering, but it seemed to work for him too.

We were in the two-and-tuppeny seats, which was luxury as I did not have to crane my neck to follow the story.

What struck me most about the evening was a short film about Italy, most of which I could not follow. Suddenly on the screen was the naked body of Mussolini, hanging upside down from a petrol pump. Somebody laughed and I felt sick. Why would they do that to anyone? The image faded and the commentator droned on in his metallic voice. I felt ashamed that such a thing could happen to a human being and that people would stand by and watch. I thought then of the dead jackdaws and knew that I would steal no more strawberries.

Six

A spring issued from the base of the hill and trickled in a rivulet into the marsh to lose itself in a wilderness of yellow flag irises and tall rushes. It was not easy to see exactly where the spring began because of the tall grasses that virtually choked it but even in high summer, when dust covered the hedgerows, it persisted, a flash of startling green where you could always be sure to see a frog going about his business with a calm air of wisdom and repletion. I imagined that somewhere inside the hill, a great block of ice was dwindling, century by century, yielding its pent-up water to the outside world.

I wondered if I was going as daft as Mr O'Meara in entertaining such ideas. Had the ice a spirit of its own, a personal baal, that pined for the great white wilderness and wept its tears into the green countryside? 'Not finished yet. Not finished yet.' Fanciful nonsense.

"Daydreaming again." The challenging voice startled me. "What are you moping about now?"

She had come upon me silently and I started.

"I'm not moping," I said defensively. "I was watching a frog."

She laughed. "A busy man."

I had to smile although I felt a bit sheepish. I always seemed to see her in sunshine and when I least expected to.

She hunkered down beside me and looked into the wet grass. "He'd know a thing or two about this place."

"Who?"

"The frog. I dare say he's been around a long time. It's very handy being small and green."

She drew her hand slowly through the water.

"It's funny," I volunteered, "but I was just thinking about all that, how this place began, like."

"How do you mean?"

"Well, the Ice Age and all that."

"You're quite a scholar, aren't you?" It was not said derisively but I could not be quite sure if it was a compliment spoken like a jeer or vice versa.

Book-learning seemed somehow inadequate. Things learnt in school are for school alone. Nobody really believes them in the outside world.

"Tell me a bit more then," she urged even though I knew that she had probably studied the same stuff herself. I told her about Mr O'Meara and his theories, being careful to laugh, making it quite clear that I did not take him seriously.

"He's a bit of a poet, your Mr O'Meara, isn't he?" she remarked after a while. "It's a pity he ended up as a school teacher."

A fate worse than death, oblivion. I suppose at that very moment, Mr O'Meara was doing a spot of weeding and in imagination, hacking his way through the rain drenched forests of New Guinea. She sat back and clasped her hands around her knees.

"I'll let you into a secret," she said meditatively.

"What is it?" I asked.

"Take your time. Take your time. Secrets aren't to be given away just like that."

"Oh," I said abashed. I sat quiet, afraid to startle her or frighten her off whatever the confidence might be.

"Do you ever imagine that you have been somewhere before?"

"Yes, sometimes. You think you've done exactly the same thing some other time."

"No, not quite like that. I know that feeling too. No." She paused. "This is different. I feel that I used to live here a long time ago, that this hill belonged to me and all my family lived here."

I could feel a grin pulling at the corners of my mouth. It always happens at the wrong time.

"Now, you're laughing at me," she said and made to rise. With a shock I saw that there were tears in her eyes.

"No, no, I'm sorry. I just thought of something else. I wasn't laughing at you," I added quickly, afraid that she would go.

"What was that?"

"Just you used to say that your ancestors were all witches and fairies. Maybe they all lived here," I laughed, going along with the yarn but she remained serious.

"I know the Sheehys lived here once but something happened and we lost the hill. I'm sure of it. That's why I keep coming back here."

I felt like an intruder. She had withdrawn into herself. There was a faraway look in her eye.

"Maybe there are some documents," I suggested.

She smiled then, as one smiles at the simple-minded.

"They didn't have documents then, not in oul' god's time."

The phrase stuck in my mind. Had she said 'the oul' god's time'? It was a well known expression but I wondered about it afterwards.

"Well anyway, there's not much you can do about it at this stage, is there? Not without documents."

I had considerable faith in documents. There was an old book at home, *The People's Law Book,* which I had dipped into occasionally, revelling in the quaint language. 'Ignorance of the law is no excuse for a breach thereof,' it proclaimed on the title page. It was particularly good on trespass. 'Tender the landowner a shilling', was its recommendation in such circumstances, provided of course, no damage had been done, even — and here was the catch — to the extent of bending a blade of grass. Few mortals were immune. I glanced to see if the grass where Kate sat had been flattened and indeed it was. She caught my glance and plucked the hem of her skirt, perhaps mistaking my train of thought.

"You'll have to make money then, and buy it back," I suggested.

"Oh no, Badger would never sell. It was too hard for them to hold onto it all this time.'

"Well that's it then," I said airily. "Isn't it?"

"Oh, I'll get it back," she replied. "There are ways and means."

"You could put a spell on him," I suggested.

"I could that," she agreed and laughed again.

I stood up and stretched.

"There is one thing you could do for me," she said.

"What?"

"You could find the key to the old house. It must be around somewhere. I want to get inside."

"Are you nuts?" I said incredulously. "Badger would kill you, and me too which is worse."

"You just get me the key, little boy, if you're not too scared."

I snorted contemptuously. "If there's a key I'll get it, you needn't worry. In fact, I'd fancy a squint in there myself."

Again she looked at me quizzically and I knew she was impressed. The man against the sky. I drew myself to my full height.

"O.K. then," she said offhand. "And by the way, you don't have to buy any more strawberries. They're always mushed by lunchtime."

I could feel my face burning with embarrassment. Indeed I had been buying strawberries and in truth, they seeped out through the *aspro* bag, long before lunch time. I was ashamed of my scruples. There is something grand indeed about larceny but petty honesty is as petty as theft.

"Ah," I said, at a loss for words.

"Never mind," she said with mockery in her eyes, "you can make amends by stealing the key."

It seemed that I was forgiven.

On a bronze coloured afternoon near the end of summer, Badger and a couple of workmen set fire to the hill. The flames grasped at the gorse and suddenly the hill was engulfed in a crackling, exploding conflagration that drew onlookers from miles away. Smoke rolled into the sky, and the landscape beyond danced and shimmered like a mirage. Wherever the fire died down momentarily, a sudden gust of wind would bring it back with intense heat. The tall, bare stalks snapped angrily and succumbed into piles of glowing charcoal. The terriers, comical in their excitement, made great sport among the small animals that fled in terror from the blaze.

"There's caves under that moat," said Badger pensively, stepping on a small flicker of fire that had crept downhill. "That's where the vermin are." He spat into the blackened grass. "The fire is the only man to get rid of them."

By evening the hill stood scorched and shorn, and the naked rim of the fort was visible through skeletal stalks. By nightfall it was a black dome with here and there, the ruby glow of a few last embers.

After the initial excitement, the episode left me feeling depressed. It was inconceivable that anything green could ever again take root in that blasted wasteland. That summer place of fantasy and secret longing was destroyed beyond redemption. I was almost glad at the thought of returning to school.

In the meantime there was still the problem of the key. She had asked me about it several times and had given me a peculiar look, a mixture of irritation and contempt. It was all very well for her but I could hardly case the joint with the old woman always around. Even when I carried water into the scullery for her, she kept a sharp eye on me and I had no doubt that the Civic Guards would be called in if she found me rooting around in the kitchen drawers or wherever. Eventually however, I located it at the back of a deep ledge over the kitchen range. It was about eight inches long and heavy enough to be used as a weapon. It had to be the right one. It was too big by far for the cottage door.

The old woman, moving as if on casters in her long black dress, challenged me.

"What are ye doin' there?"

"Nothing," I replied with a guilty start. "I was only looking at the picture." The Sacred Heart stared at me, seeing into my soul and the lie that lurked there. He looked very sad, as who would not with his heart outside his shirt.

"Well get on owa' that and do your work," she muttered, straightening with difficulty to glance along the shelf. Nothing had been disturbed.

I formulated a brilliant plan to substitute another key. There were lots of old keys around the station. I selected the nearest one in size from a ring that hung on the back of the kitchen door and, at great personal risk, made the substitution. A man on a galloping horse would never notice the difference.

I believe my father raised Cain and resorted to some serious profanity at having to smash the lock on the turf shed when the cold weather came back but by that time I was well out of earshot.

It pelted rain for the last week or two of the holidays. The swamp filled up and overflowed, turning the neighbouring fields to quagmires. I asked her brothers about Kate and they told me that she had been ill and had not been out since the fire on the hill.

"Yeah," grumbled one of the smallest ones, looking out from under his sou'wester, "she kept me awake with her nightmares. Some people have no consideration."

The hill was veiled in rain and disconsolately I prepared for school. I put the key in my suitcase for safe keeping and only as the train was pulling out did the sky break and the rain lifted. I could see in the weak sunlight, that a faint gauze of green had re-established itself on the wizened summit.

Father Rice expatiated on the great migrations of ancient times and how the Romans tried, like the little boy at the dyke but less effectively, to plug the breaches in their boundaries. The prelude to this great explosion of population out of Asia was the descent of the Celts upon Rome and the sack of that city, although to be absolutely fair, the Romans were immigrants themselves and had wrested the land from earlier inhabitants. It was a bit like coming out of mass, in that those in front were an impediment to progress, while those behind were an inexorable force always pushing forward and treading on heels.

The geese of course, saved Rome and the senators kept their dignity, if not their heads, but the Celts moved on. Rome was not to their liking and perhaps a century or so later the great grandchildren of those country bumpkins who had gazed in awe at the big city arrived at last at their island of destiny, whither of course they had been heading all along. This he called the heroic age, the age of iron and chariots and of superhuman warrior kings.

It seemed to me like a dark and jagged time when head-hunting and theft were regarded as gentlemanly pursuits. Looking down the long corridor of history it appeared to be strewn with mutilated corpses, heads on spikes, unspeakable punishment of those who questioned or stepped out of line. Carnage was justified and became laudable depending on who was telling the tale. Treachery when the others did it, masterly strategy when we notched up a few scores. Livy whinged when Hannibal pulled a fast one, but he swelled with pride when 'our men' caused a great slaughter of the enemy.

These things having been perceived, as it were, I questioned Father Rice on the notions of fair play and decency which he frequently enjoined upon his pupils. "Ah," he said and paused, turning a long stick of chalk between his fingers, "a valid point. I suppose, because it all happened so long ago and is described with such clarity and style, we can take a more objective view. Even in the darkest times battles were fought according to set rules of etiquette. The ancient peoples were very conscious of the force of law, in their own terms, of course." He smiled fleetingly. "No doubt if we were to behave in the same manner nowadays a very dim view would be taken of it."

There was a murmur of amusement and some sword play broke out at the back of the class, which was quickly brought under control.

"In fact, that Brennus, as the Romans called him, who led his people into Rome, was certainly a Celtic Brehon, a law-giver. They merely mistook the title for a name. Anyway," he went on, picking up another thread, "their arrival in Ireland more or less marks the beginning of our Iron Age and the establishment of a Celtic ruling class on this island, which was to last in some degree, down to the time of the plantations."

He was off again on another tack but I had seized on his explanation of Brennus, a figure shrouded in mystery, a judge, law-giver, warrior wandering in quest of a home. Brennus, brehon, Brehony. Had his descendants found it at last on that hill beside the forest which exercised such a fascination for me?

The sack of Rome they called it, and Badger undoubtedly knew a thing or two about sacks. Perhaps his ancestors had carried off their loot in hessian sacks, hence the term, with 'swag', printed on them in the best cartoon traditions. I began to smile at the idea and Father Rice was onto me like a shot.

"And what might be amusing you, young man?"

"Nothing, Father." It would be too difficult to explain.

"So you're smiling at nothing." He raised his eyebrows. "You are to be pitied." He turned away but as an afterthought, added softly, almost to himself, "On second thoughts, perhaps you are to be envied."

The smell of cabbage, running ahead of the bell, summoned us to dinner and saved me from any further embarrassment.

Like commercial travellers we lived out of our suitcases. Anything of value was kept locked away under the bed although we did risk hanging up a few clothes. Subconsciously, as long as the suitcase contained some items, it meant that we had not unpacked, therefore we were not staying permanently; we were going home. Mine contained among other things, a scout knife with all the gear, even a spoon. There were a few American comics, contraband, in which the females were equipped with spectacular breasts, barely restrained by bizarre leather or metal outfits which drew attention to what they concealed. Quite a number of these women were villains but I was prepared to overlook their small faults in consideration of their obvious virtues. American comics were like gold dust in our ascetic and sexless existence but had to be read circumspectly for fear of the prowling Father McBride.

I also had a chart showing the various options open to the cricket captain in placing his fielders — not a lot of practical use in my circumstances but very clear and neatly illustrated nonetheless. I had had a few offers for it but was holding out for a better price. There was also a chest expander that did not work. It carried a money back guarantee — which reminds me.

On the bottom of the case, under all this stuff was the key. I often took it out and looked at it. Could it be the key to all the mysteries of life? It would give me access to a secret place where presumably no one had been for a hundred years. It would be our place, Kate's and mine, hidden from the world, where we could be as one. It would bring us irrevocably together. My imagination became heated at the contemplation of a kind of clandestine domestic bliss.

Maybe I thought about it too much, because if anyone saw me with the key I blushed and hid it away. It was always at the back of my mind and came between me and my studies. Sometimes I dreamed about the key and the old house and Kate waiting there for me with open arms, her blouse unbuttoned and white thighs showing through the scantiest of costumes — the whole works, in stark chiaroscuro, like the comic book heroines. It got to the point where I could conjure up the vision at any time and mentally absented myself from many a tedious class, closing the door of our secret place behind us. It earned me a good few clips in the ear and consistently falling grades.

One night the dream was different. There was fire. We ran from the hill into the woods. There were old people and children screaming. I heard shouts and laughter and the belling of hounds. Black figures darted about, silhouetted against the flames. Kate ran towards me, her mouth like a black hole and her eyes white with terror. I reached for her but she eluded me. I searched for her through the wood. The shouts receded and the flames became a distant flicker through the undergrowth. She was gone. A frog said, "Wake up."

"Shut up, you fool," grumbled a voice sleepily.

"Yeah. Shut up," agreed a second.

I turned on my side and drew the blankets around me. The darkness seethed all about. I pulled my feet well in and wrapped the blankets tight. The nameless terror under the bed cannot get you if your feet are in and your eyes are shut. That is a well known fact. I closed my eyes and eventually drifted back to sleep.

Seven

Holly and ivy; green boughs; in the dead of winter: Tom bears logs into the hall. Images of Christmas from another time and another place, almost become our own.

We always went to Olford Hall for a bundle of holly. At sixpence it was good value as long as there were plenty of berries.

"Make sure there are plenty of berries," was my mother's parting advice, "and mind your manners." There was the old vestigial respect for the gentry. 'Mind your manners.' There was also a resentment, a 'let's show them that we are no ignorant clodhoppers' attitude. 'Mind your manners. Don't be bold.' Bold, brave, courageous, and therefore a challenge, a danger to the established scheme of things. If knights had not been bold where would we be today?

The rutted gravel avenue curved through woodland towards the old house. It seemed to me like a foreign country, not the familiar pasture and plough land outside the perimeter woods, but a rolling English parkland with copses and plantations, cover for game, a carefully planned naturalness, alien enough to make us tread carefully and keep to the path.

'Ringing of the merry bells, and the running of the deer.' This would be the place, I thought. Will Shakespeare himself and Sir John Falstaff would have been at home there, keeping Yuletide cheer at Olford Hall.

"Watch out," said Fergal, pulling me suddenly off the track.

A motorcycle sped around a bend in a flurry of gravel, almost speedway style. I caught a glimpse of the rider's eyes through angled goggles and he was gone. We turned to watch enviously.

"Did you not hear him coming?" asked Anto accusingly. "Were you day-dreaming as usual?"

"'Course I heard him," I mumbled, adding truculently, "why should I have to get out of the way?"

"Because you'd be killed. That's why," scoffed Anto with incontrovertible logic.

There was no answer to that. We went around to the yard but there was nobody about.

"Maybe we should go round to the front door," suggested Anto.

It seemed a bit presumptuous, but why not? At anyone else's house we would have gone to the front door. Centuries of inherited diffidence. Fergal, as the eldest took the responsibility of knocking. The noise echoed inside the old house and eventually we heard someone approaching the door. It was old Mr Olford himself, a tall thin man with round spectacles and sparse grey hair.

"Gentlemen," he said affably enough. "What can I do for you?"

"We wonder if you could oblige with some holly." Fergal got it out perfectly. 'Oblige with some holly' — a nice touch.

"Certainly," the old man replied. "Was there no one to look after you?" He frowned. This would not do. A regrettable lapse on the part of the servants. He clicked his tongue in annoyance.

"Step in, gentlemen, while I find a pair of wellingtons."

He shuffled off in his carpet slippers and we looked about us. The hall was stone flagged, with old black furniture, a table, a large sideboard sort of thing and a subsiding leather sofa with much of its horsehair peering through seams. The walls were the most startling feature of all, lined with rows of animal trophies: kudu, eland, buffalo, gazelle, each one identified, with its place of demise stated on a small brass plaque. Shot by J. Olford, German East Africa 1912. Shot by J. Olford, Matabeleland 1910. Shot by J. Olford, Kenya 1913, and so on, where and when, but never why.

We stared about us in awe. The animals regarded us proudly with sightless glass eyes. Dust had settled upon them. A lion glared down from the first landing. I could have sworn that a springbok twitched as if ready for flight. My heart ached for the oldness, the seedy elegance of the place, for a world long vanished.

The old man came back presently and clumped ahead of us along the drive and into the stable yard. A horse stirred in a loose-box, trying the door with a tap of its hoof.

"Somebody should have been here to look after you," he said again, leading us into a shed piled high with holly. He took out a small curved penknife and cut a length of binder twine.

"Take as much as you like," he said and handed me the cord.

We thanked him and Fergal diffidently produced the sixpence. The old man slipped it into his waistcoat pocket, thumbing it safely into place.

"A nice old bloke, all the same," said Fergal as we trudged homewards, taking turns to shoulder the bundle.

"I was a bit surprised he took the tanner, though," said Anto, "though I suppose business is business."

I said nothing, although I had thought he might have been insulted.

"They used to have everything up there," continued Fergal, "race horses, tennis courts, all that sort of thing, I believe. Big parties an' all." The mighty had indeed fallen.

"They lost a lot of money in Africa."

"Yeah, the Mau Mau," said Anto enthusiastically. That explained everything. I was never too keen on the Mau Mau, particularly since my brothers had long ago told me gleefully about the Night of the Long Knives, when all Europeans would die in their beds. It had never happened of course, but I had looked carefully at the map on the classroom wall to reassure myself that we were in the most distant corner of Europe. Somebody would surely have put a stop to it before the Mau Mau, creeping through the darkness with their pangas, could reach Ireland. They still lurked there somewhere in the depths of my mind.

We went down through the woods and cut across the fields to the station.

The afternoon sun threw a long shadow below Brehonys' hill and the windows of the haunted house glinted orange in the gloom. A shotgun sound in the marsh reverberated over the frost bound fields.

"It's the Mau Mau," said Anto and we laughed. It was the midwinter day. Soon people would remark on the brave stretch in the evenings.

The snow came after Christmas, a violent night of wind and eerie brightness and in the morning a landscape transformed. Drifts slanted against walls and hedges and trains were delayed. We trekked about, engaging in battles with anyone we met, or tobagganning on the real stuff for a change. There was a compulsion to leave tracks on any unmarked expanse of snow, to run in a spiral into the middle of a white plain and step out backwards, putting the feet carefully into the crisp, deep footprints so that everyone would wonder where you had vanished to. In the same way I suppose, an artist regards a white canvas.

It was a suitable time to make an expedition to Barneville Castle, a place of high adventure and romance for many generations of children and courting couples. From the top of the bell tower you could see into five counties. Wicklow shrouded in white loomed in the distance. A blanket of white stretched, interminable, into Meath and Louth. The Mournes marched along the northern horizon. We could trace our own footprints stretching back through the field and along the side of the road. Far away we could see small black figures running about and their cries came thinly to us on our lofty eminence.

Anto scraped a drift of powdery snow from the ledge and watched it disintegrate and drift down on the breeze.

"Just think. If you had a rifle up here you could really let them have it." He sighted along an imaginary barrel.

"Who?" queried Fergal.

"Well anyone," said Anto airily. "I mean, if you had to." He squeezed off a couple of shots. "The perfect target."

"Missed," jeered Fergal. "They're still moving."

"I wasn't aiming," maintained the marksman. "If I wanted to I could drop the Sheehy tribe in their tracks."

I looked again with keener interest. I could recognise Kate now and my heart gave a jump.

"Let's go down and ambush them," suggested Anto but Fergal demurred. "That wouldn't be fair. They're only kids and she's a girl."

He was always very observant, I reflected. Nevertheless they went down. I could hear them slipping and swearing on the spiral stairs.

After a while I heard someone climbing the steps and eventually a woolly hat emerged, followed by Kate Sheehy, red in the face and panting. The tip of her nose shone brightly, a sign of health, in dogs at least. Snowflakes clung to the wool of her hat, where my brothers had momentarily forgotten the deference due to ladies, or maybe, as I reasoned later, they had been paying her the oblique compliments of the inarticulate. She drew in a deep breath and laughed.

"That's a terrible climb. It always gives me cramps in the legs."

She stamped on the little platform and the snow squeaked under her boots. "Have you been up here long?"

"A good while," I said. "It's quite a sight, isn't it?"

She looked around, turning slowly through three hundred and sixty degrees, taking in the whole scene. A tremor passed through her body, possibly from the biting wind.

"It's beautiful," she said softly after a while, "so clean, almost untouched."

I followed her gaze to where the distant hedgerows foreshortened to become a dense black forest, standing starkly out of the dazzling white.

"Imagine living here," I interjected. "Think of the feeling of power, looking down on everyone."

"They must have been very frightened all the time, to build such big walls," she said thoughtfully.

I had never thought of it that way.

"Thomas de Barneville," she said. "Did you ever hear tell of him? He built this as his stronghold."

"Vaguely," I answered, peeved. I was supposed to be the expert.

"He built this place, all right. He took the land from the Seagraves, Norsemen."

"Is that so?" I was impressed. "How do you know all that?"

"Oh, I read books too, you know," she replied airily. "You're not the only one." I was wrongfooted again. "Of course, my grandfather used to know all the old stories about this part of the world. He told me about the de Barnevilles. There were still some of that family living around here in his time. Some relation to the Olfords."

"That would have been, what, eight hundred years after this place was built," I said in astonishment.

"That's right," she agreed. "My grandfather went to their house once looking for work at the threshing and old Barnwell asked him for his pedigree. 'Me what?' says Grandad. 'Your pedigree,' says old Barnwell."

"What did he mean?" I queried.

"Oh, references and that kind of thing. Anyway, Grandad had no idea what he meant, so he went off and went into a pub and had a few drinks. They were telling him in the pub all about old Barnwell and what a mean old so and so he was."

"Then what happened?"

"Well Grandad went back again in the afternoon and out comes your man and says 'Well, have you got your pedigree yet?' Grandad had a good few in him and he says, 'No, I haven't, but I've got yours, you mean oul' bastard.'" She laughed at the recollection.

"That Barnwell was the last of that family around here. Funny, isn't it?" I looked down again into the remains of the courtyard and tried to imagine de Barneville and his men preparing to ride out to impose their iron will on the countryside. Horses, amoeba like, seen from above, shuffled and stamped on the flagstones and armour clinked and creaked as men shifted in their saddles. The stronghold of de Barneville indeed.

"A cold old place, though," I surmised.

"Your nose has gone purple," she pointed out. "You look like a boozer."

"I have the key, by the way," I said anxious to cut a more imposing figure in her eyes. "The key of the old house."

"The key? Oh yes, that. I had nearly forgotten about that." She was perhaps a little too casual.

"We could try it, I suppose, whenever the snow melts." My words hung in the chilly air and I held my breath.

"Why when the snow melts?" she asked, puzzled.

"Tracks," I explained. "you don't want to leave tracks, do you?" Kit Carson would not have needed any explanation.

"Who cares?" she said dismissively, "But maybe you're right. I tell you what, you let me know when you think it's a good time."

"Right," I said and prayed for a Chinook to come and melt away the tell-tale snow. The Chinook, Snow-Eater of the High Plains. *National Geographic* to the rescue again.

"What are we doing standing here?" she said, "I'm frozen to the bone." I had barely noticed the stinging wind, and would have stayed aloft there forever, like St. Simeon but with better reason.

"Make yourself useful," my father said, handing me a navvy, a broad square shovel of the type used by the firemen, "and scrape all the snow off the platform." In those less litigious times a customer could come a cropper at his own expense, but it was no harm to shift the compacted snow from the brink of the platform. There was the vertiginous drop between platform and carriage, a twelve inch wide abyss which conjured up pictures of mangled legs and wallets irrevocably lost. Old ladies trembled over it and children were drawn to it as if by a magnet.

"What did a fellow say to me the other morning?" said my father as I scraped away. A rhetorical opening.

"What?" I asked, as required.

"Well he came down in a heap on the steps and nearly broke his snitch." Sketching in the background, setting the scene. The snitch, that most frequently injured part of the body, is not specifically mentioned in first-aid manuals.

"What did he say?" I persisted, jabbing at the snow. My father smiled and stuck his hands into his trousers pockets.

"'Tom,' says he, 'it's a hard oul' station.'"

"Get ah'd'vit," I retorted and flicked a lump of snow at him. He skipped back adroitly and stood there chuckling.

I scraped on.

"Why do they call this a navvy?" I asked after a while.

"They used them when they were building the railways. The men were called navigators."

"Navigators! I mean you'd hardly lose your way in a train, would you?"

"I suppose not," he conceded.

The signal wires rattled in the culvert.

"Twenty past four," he mused aloud. "I wonder if Badger is on it." I stopped and leaned on the shovel in the regulation fashion.

"Why?"

"He went in this morning. I just figure he should be back about now." It wasn't that he was inquisitive about other people's business but he liked a sense of completeness about things, loose ends tied up, doors clicked shut, that sort of thing.

"I often meant to ask," I said, "why was he called Badger anyway?"

"Ahh," he said rubbing the side of his nose. "That's a long story."

"Why, though?" I pressed. "Was it like, a family nickname like Foxy Blake?" A long line of Blakes had rejoiced in the title Foxy, aptly named too. The Blakes, it was said, would mind mice at a cross-roads and put feet under ducks. This last was the essence of cuteness, so much so that I never even knew what it meant.

"Ah no," he said with a rueful grin. "I suppose I must take a share of the blame. You see, his wife gave him a terrible time. I shouldn't speak ill of the dead I suppose, but she was a right hairpin. Poor Badger, she used to scrab the face off him. You'd see him some days and you'd think he'd spent the night nosing through brambles like a badger. It sort of caught on."

"Could he not stop her?"

"Ah, Badger couldn't handle her at all, at all. He never understood women. He's too gentle altogether." He sniffed and drew the back of his hand across his nose. "They have to know who's boss."

I wondered about that. If my father was boss, I dare say my mother had never noticed.

"What happened to her, anyway?"

"A townswoman she was. She just didn't belong. She never made a go of it."

"She died."

"Aye. There was some talk about doing herself in, but I wouldn't put much pass on that."

I shivered. He had planted the seed of curiosity nonetheless. I could hardly ask Badger about her though.

The familiar rumbling of the train interrupted our conversation and my father hurried towards the tunnel steps. In a minute he appeared on the down platform, stalking majestically and twitching the hem of his tunic, the embodiment of the Great Northern Railway.

I was conscious of eyes watching me as the train pulled in. I was a bit player in the great tableau that entertains the railway traveller, a snippet of life glimpsed for a moment and never seen again, like the sheep caught in the wire, the angler on the viaduct, the horses kicking up their heels, pretending to be terrified by the smoke, the golfer, pausing in his serious deliberations.

I pondered Lil' Abner's legitimate concern that the train 'might jes' come through sideways,' while he 'wuz standin' on the platfoam.' Deep thoughts went on in that pointed head. I kept my head down so no one could see me smirking to myself and I scraped on diligently. Prince Henry the Navvy. It lacked a certain dignity. The train groaned and clanked and pulled away in a cloud of steam. My father and Badger were talking on the opposite platform. I noted the neat brown-paper parcels and the Guiney's bag under Badger's oxter. After a few minutes they separated and Badger headed off across the fields dwindling like a straggler from a Breughel landscape.

I lay in bed wondering what would happen if the snow simply decided to stay. Supposing it became the norm and was replenished. Supposing our familiar fields and houses were obliterated under drifting blankets of snow and we burrowed out each day to try to carry on. Surely the government would have to do something. It would be quite a problem but who could say that it could never happen?

I woke to the sound of running water, a fugue for down pipes and gully trap. I could see the train travellers stepping gingerly between ridges of grey brown slush. Galoshes were much in evidence. The air was warm and the snow was shrinking visibly under the bright morning sun. Dvoràk's Slavs were prancing merrily in the kitchen and blasts of static told me that the iron was plugged in.

'And every day brought forth a noble deed.'

I slipped the key into my jacket pocket and headed downstairs to see what the day might have in store for me.

Eight

I considered it wise to wait almost till dusk before getting into the old house. We were standing among the pines waiting until the coast was completely clear. One of the labourers went past, taking the cattle indoors. The hooves made sucking sounds as they squelched through the mud. The man cursed absentmindedly and slapped the hindmost animal with an ash plant. Splatters of dung belied their elegant gait and lady-like demeanour.

"At least Badger is out of the way," I whispered drawing Kate back behind a tree.

"How do you make that out?" she queried.

"Well his old Volks was up at your place, wasn't it?"

"Oh yea, but he gets Da to do a job on it now and again, that's all. In fact he lends it to him whenever he wants it."

That surprised me. "I didn't think they were such pals."

"That's the funny thing," she whispered. "He's got very matey all of a sudden."

"Hmm," I mused, "so he's not necessarily out of the way then. We'd better be careful then."

She nodded and bit her lip. I could see that she was more nervous than she admitted.

"Let's get on with it," I whispered and bending low, headed for the door. There was an iron bar set athwart the doorway and wedged into the stone architrave with beaten lead. In itself it presented no great problem, provided the lock could be turned.

The key grated as if in sand as I turned it tentatively. I felt Kate's hand gripping my arm.

"Go on," she said again but there was no movement.

"The springs must have given up the ghost," I suggested and immediately regretted my words.

"Here, let me try," she said impatiently and reached across me. There was a click and a snap and suddenly the door moved.

"It works," I said unnecessarily as the hinges protested. I had seen this kind of scene time and again in the films. There should have been a cadaverous footman, his face lit eerily from below, to intone 'Your rooms are ready,' as a prelude to a night of terror, but there was nothing.

I ducked under the bar and pushed the door open wider. The hallway was bare boards, lit by a grimy fanlight and a small round window at the turn of the stairs. Distemper had blossomed with the damp into a chemical garden of salts.

A fine dust covered everything.

"Hey, this is great," I whispered. Through an open door I could see where a mountain of twigs had accumulated in the hearth, spilling over onto a flagged kitchen floor. There was an old fashioned crook and a bellows crank set into the wall.

"Jackdaws," I said knowledgeably. "This isn't a bit spooky." I consider myself particularly sensitive to atmosphere. No answer came from behind me. I looked around. Kate stood at the open door, her hands on the bar, frozen in mute terror.

"What's wrong? What's wrong?" I said alarmed. The blood had drained from her face. She looked like a ghost.

She made no sound. Her eyes stared but she did not appear to see me.

"What's wrong?" I said again. "It's o.k. There's nothing there."

Her head twitched and her lips moved but no sound came. I thought of epilepsy and incongruously of a ruler to hold her tongue. That was what a teacher had done to a lad in school. I can't imagine what help a foot of hairy timber stuffed down your gullet might be in an emergency. Anyway I had no ruler.

I tried talking to her softly, beginning to be frightened myself at the thought that somebody might come along and catch us breaking and entering.

"Come on," I said, ducking out under the bar. "We'll leave it alone for now."

It was as if she had been welded to the bar. I tried to prise her fingers free but as quickly as I released one hand the other grasped it again with a desperate tenacity. Eventually I put both arms around her, and, levering both hands free at the same time, pulled her away from the doorway. It occurred to me that it was the first time I had put my arms around a girl with any serious intent. It was a pleasant sensation, despite my alarm. I was tempted to prolong the situation but she stumbled away from me and sat down on the crumbling bole of a fallen tree.

With an instinct for self-preservation, I pulled the door to. The lock snapped shut with no difficulty. I went back to her. She was staring at her hands.

"Burned me," she whimpered, like a child. "Burned me."

I crouched down and took both her hands in mine, uncertain whether to humour her or scoff at her cowardice. At least this time I had come off best for a change. With admirable daring I raised her fingers to my lips and kissed them lightly.

"There now," I said, "that will make them better."

My levity had no effect. She sat as if stunned, rocking slightly to and fro.

Christ, I thought, what am I going to do? I was tempted to leave her there, rationalising that she would be all right after a while. There was no point in both of us being caught. There was something about massaging the blood towards the heart. That was it. I should take her pulse. I put my hand inside her coat and felt the wool of her jumper. There was definitely a pulse. There was something else as well, a warm soft mound, a breast, I surmised. My hand strayed over it. Yes, it definitely was a breast. My theoretical knowledge stood me in good stead. There should be another one on the other side. I felt the blood pounding in my temples. Supposing we both died at that very moment. It would be very difficult to explain what was going on. Slowly and reluctantly I withdrew my hand. She would probably live and so would I, but would I ever walk again? That problem of uncalled for erection dogged me for many a long year and occasionally required me to adopt the guise of an incurable arthritic, when alighting from a bus or train. An old war wound or sports injury will also fill the bill. I read somewhere that Socrates, I think it was, on his seventieth birthday, cried 'Free at last.' His wife was a bit of a hairpin too it seems.

Not all of these thoughts went through my mind at that precise time. It was more an amalgam of guilt and exhilaration and the fear of what she might say.

I massaged her hands, studiously avoiding looking her in the face. Presently she spoke again.

"Didn't you hear them?" she said and her voice trembled.

"Who? Hear who?" My voice squeaked from feigned nonchalance. "I didn't hear anyone." I looked around. To be branded both as a housebreaker and degenerate in the one day would have been too much for my sorrowing parents.

The pine boughs sighed overhead as the wind rustled through them. I was conscious of a smell of damp pine-needles and mouldering wood.

"There's no one around," I said with relief. "We're all right."

"Did you not hear the people crying in the house?"

My skin prickled all over.

"No," I said stoutly. "There was nobody there."

"In the house," she insisted. "There were people crying." Tears began to run down her face. "I heard them," she said again urgently. "I heard them." I said nothing. I noticed that I was still holding her hands. I wondered how to let go. In the films the hero produces a gleaming white handkerchief from his breast pocket in such situations. This I could not do for reasons which I need not dwell upon. Gently I brushed some of the tears from her cheeks with my fingertips. Gradually her colour returned.

"We'd better go," I said eventually.

"Look," she said, holding out her hands, palms upwards. There were what appeared to be red weals where she had gripped the bar.

"They're hurting," she whimpered, like a child.

I looked more closely and rather impatiently.

"That's only rust," I said dismissively. "It's only the cold that's stinging."

I wiped some of the rust off but a stain remained.

She stooped down and picked up a smooth green stone that had been cast up by the tree's roots, a dark polished pebble with flecks of light in it like seeds of fire.

Slowly she turned it between her hands.

"Come on," I said. "Let's go."

She made no objection. The dry sticks of cowparsley snapped under our feet. She seemed preoccupied and followed me without comment slowly turning the stone in the palm of one hand and then transferring it to the other.

"You go up through the wood," I said. "You won't meet anyone at this hour." She nodded and I left her at the stile that let into the pathway through the trees. I headed off quickly in the opposite direction. When I looked back from a distance of a couple of fields there was a man talking to her at the stile. It was Badger. There was no mistaking the old macintosh. No doubt she could give him a plausible story. There was no cause for alarm. I went on through the soaking grass thinking about the events of the afternoon. I concluded that she was an actress, an attention seeker. She must have known all along that my hand was inside her coat. She must have wanted me to do it and that was why she said nothing. What a yarn about being burned and ghosts inside the house! She was scared of the house but not that scared. I had her figured out. She was trying to lure me in to greater intimacies. Maybe I should have played along a bit harder just to see how far she would go. There would undoubtedly be other times though, now that I knew the score. I began to laugh aloud. What a chancer! She would never fool me again. I broke into a trot, shadow-boxing the air. If Marciano had crossed my path just then he was a goner.

On the last Sunday before returning to school I sat in the chapel and looked at Kate Sheehy in the front pew. I thought about her body. I knew that I would go to Hell for such thoughts, but there and then, it was worth it. I vowed to stop during the Consecration, as a gesture of goodwill. Obviously, I thought wryly, she was no witch anyway. A witch could probably grasp red-hot iron with no bother.

There was a stir in the chapel, a whispering and shuffling of feet. I looked around to see Badger and his mother arriving. She was her usual self, with, if it were possible, an even darker glare than normal, but Badger was got up in a very snappy double-breasted suit with a shirt of oxblood stripes. He carried a new hat and gloves. It was, as they say, far from gloves he was reared. I stared as he slipped self-consciously into his seat. Except for the shoes he looked like a minor gangster. The shoes were brown brogues with punched designs on them and bright yellow soles that did not hide just a smidgin of cowdung under the instep. He had a kind of self satisfied smirk and occasionally brushed the nap of his hat with his cuff. I noticed a fleck of paper under his chin where he had cut himself, a miniature Japanese flag. He was not as old looking as I had always assumed.

The priest arrived in a flourish of vestments. He glared around until there was silence and then sucking air through his thin lips impatiently, he began the mass.

This sartorial display was the subject of much discussion at breakfast. Sunday being a slack day, my father liked to linger over his fry, discussing the agenda for the day, drinking innumerable cups of tea and piling impossible mounds of marmalade onto his toast.

"He's a new man, right enough." I could swear there was a touch of mockery, even malice when he caught my eye. "They tell me he has a great notion of Kate Sheehy, God knows he's up there often enough. Sure Dan has the use of the old Volks more than himself – fixing it moryah."

The room darkened and swam around me. I heard my mother's dismissive tones, but could not make out what she said. I could not swallow what I had been chewing. They were looking at me and talking all at the same time. I could feel cold sweat like a moustache on my lip. I raised a hand to wipe it away.

"Probably the climb, on an empty stomach," my father was saying. He looked concerned.

"I'm all right," I mumbled and took a swig of tea to help me swallow. My appetite was gone.

"Go and lie down for a while," said my mother gently, "and then you'll have to get your stuff ready for school."

I was glad to escape to try to straighten out the absurdity of what had been suggested. My father always had a wicked sense of humour. He loved the comedians on the radio and listened carefully for the punchline. He delighted in puns and long shaggy-dog stories. This was the kind of rumour that he enjoyed passing on. If it turned out to be true he could say 'I told you so.' If not, he was still a gas man.

Disconsolately I packed my case, folding everything carefully. I took the key out of my pocket and looked at it, tempted to throw it away but fidelity is my middle name. The key was my talisman. No one could separate us as long as I held onto it. I slipped it under the clothes. She would not escape that easily.

Nine

Letters from home usually contained a ten-bob note and some useful tips about hygiene and how to succeed at study. Occasionally there were bits of news about relations or local people, which might have been of interest to adults. A cousin married that chap she had been going out with for years. I knew the cousin merely as a member of a branch of the family mentioned when family antagonisms and slights were being raked over and renewed. The chap has remained a dim and anonymous figure sighted occasionally at funerals and once at a wedding where he got stocious and photographed people with the flash gun set backwards on his camera.

They were building new houses on the Station Road. It seemed that they would cut off the view of the sea. The farmer used to say that he would never sell that field even if you covered it with fivers. Every man has his price.

My father mentioned *en passant*, that the hard Badger was ardently pressing his suit. This seemed to me the most bizarre piece of intelligence. I pictured him, in my father's phrase, a regular mickey dazzler, with knife-edged creases to his trousers. Of course he had been in the L.D.F. and the military training had probably re-asserted itself. A fellow in school showed me how his father, who was in the F.C.A. pressed his trousers, using plenty of water, brown paper and a very hot iron. It works too. Use the back of a clothes-brush to tap down the creases. Still, if Badger had spent all that money it made sense to look after his clothes. The net result was that I was being outmanoeuvred, which left me feeling very down and disconsolate.

I considered writing to her in burning, passionate phrases, declaring my undying love and devotion and pleading with her to step back from the brink, but I had no confidence in my powers of persuasion and little to offer her in exchange. When I closed my eyes I could see his broken fingernails and his hands with the scabs of many gashes, pawing at her soft young body. She could not possibly love him. It was an obscene idea. This was the spell she had once hinted at. There was no magic in it at all, just an old man making a fool of himself and a calculating little bitch. For an instant I hated her and plotted a deliciously painful death for her, in which she would at the last moment see that I was justified and would forgive me. But where would that have left me then? Perhaps I could remove Badger. An accident on a tractor. A loose safety-catch on his gun. But I knew that he was indestructible. My puny efforts would bounce off him. Ever since the day he showed me the solar-plexus punch I was wary of his physical strength. Almost like someone knuckling a barometer he rapped me on the midriff. There appeared to be no force in the blow. Electric pains shot all over my body. I could feel every little thread of nerve burning in helpless agony. I wheezed for breath and staggered about.

"Hit him on the jaw and you'll possibly break your hand," he advised earnestly. "Go for the Darby Kelly."

I wheezed some more and gradually regained control of my limbs. He had not put me down, I noted, salvaging some pride. Then again he had not really punched me either. I knew that a frontal assault would have little hope of success.

Lofty indifference, I concluded, was my best defence. Afterwards, I realised that I was thinking entirely about the effect on me. Defence is the best form of attack. I adopted a passive role, that of an observer, although I thought of myself at the time as *el Gavilan*, the hawk, circling and watching, ready to strike. *El Gavilan* was a notorious bandido I had read about in *The Wizard*. They would never know as they went about their business, that *el Gavilan* had them taped.

In practice I never liked the feeling of eavesdropping. In confession, although it would have been interesting and perhaps illuminating, to compare notes with other sinners, I coughed and creaked my knees on the bare boards, in order not to hear what was going on on the other side of the box. Greater consideration hath no man than to expend his sinovial fluid on another's behalf. All the same there were times when you could not help hearing a few goods ones. The general falling away from confession has meant that a younger generation has lost the real feel of some of the best jokes. 'And did you entertain these thoughts, my son?' 'No, but they sure entertained me.'

There lies a whole field of enquiry. I loved Kate Sheehy with all my heart. I wanted to be good and kind to her (provided I did not have to strangle her) and father her children, in due course. The thought of her made the sun shine into my life and filled me with goodwill towards all, but if I seriously devoted some time to considering what I would like to do with her or to her or whatever, a lot of which I was not too sure about, it was a sin and I had to repent of it immediately, under pain of eternal fire.

I held on and kept my counsel, waiting for the holidays to clarify the situation. In the meantime I studied Julius Caesar for my exams. Here was a cynical con-man with a nice touch in genocide, what we would probably call nowadays an entrepreneur. There was no denying that he had flair and a sense of humour and leaving aside moral issues, he had a lot of fun. In modern times we talk about the heinousness of making war on women and children. The men are left with the satisfaction of knowing that they are worthy targets. Julius had no such qualms. He believed in the final solution.

Father Rice admired his sense of order and his positive contributions to civilization but I felt sad for the Suebi, the wild people of the forest, and their children who were subject to no discipline and bathed in the rivers. I felt sorry for the Gauls and their ancient thorny fortresses, crushed under the Roman war machine. Fortunately for us though, all that kind of carry-on was finished. The natural progress of human kind was towards a stable society where law and order ruled. History was of interest largely because it showed us how far we had come: what progress we had made. It was a comforting thought. It is impossible for the young person to have any real sense of time. The couple of years in the difference between myself and Kate were a greater void than the centuries between Cromwell and Adolf Hitler. They were safely bunged away in history where they could do no further harm. The world had learned from them and would never allow such things to happen again, or so Hollywood reassured us, but meanwhile, Kate was going out to dances and was in her final year at school. Soon she would slip into the adult world while I was mired in childhood. There was no comforting notion in those days of 'teenage years' to suggest a common ground, however spurious. Panic set in when I thought about it.

In the meantime I read books and magazines. Despite all efforts to make an athlete of me, I rarely felt like running around and when I did the whole business was trammelled up in rules. The simple object of the game is complicated by a vast corpus of law, on which everyone is an expert. I have never dared to play golf for fear of being banned for life. In a sense I have shortcircuited the process. Reasonable men have come to blows over whether or not a foot was inside or outside the touchline. Mountaineers permit themselves pitons and crampons and assorted ironmongery but look down, as it were, on the use of helicopters. Logically they should climb stark-naked, without even a packet of sandwiches.

I read articles on Hitler and his war. War is a guarantee of livelihood to photographers. Hitler's side won in terms of uniforms and insignia. There was a sinister beauty about all their paraphernalia. It was easy to see why a whole nation was mesmerised by one man and his vision of an invincible state. I wondered though, why he chose the ideal of the tall fair-haired blue-eyed Aryan of which he was conspicuously not the type. Perhaps there was some modesty or diffidence about the man.

Our school history assured us that the Celts were tall, fair-haired, blue-eyed and generous, which gave us one up on the Herrenvolk. Where all their descendants had vanished to, I could not figure out. Perhaps the footnote that they disdained the use of armour, might have some bearing on the fact that Irish people nowadays come in assorted shapes and colours with no noticeable monopoly of generosity.

The concentration camps and extermination camps defied explanation. The people who built them and photographed what they did there, must have thought they were doing the right thing. If they had succeeded one hundred per cent, the matter would probably, by now, have been forgotten or even dismissed as a fabrication. But there were witnesses and survivors and the haunted faces in the photographs of the liberation. Like Macbeth's murders there were rubs and botches in the work and Fleance lived to come between the tyrant and his sleep and to become a folk memory, a child with the green bough, a nemesis. Wars and catastrophies may destroy civilizations root and branch. Old ideas will give way to new, but down through the centuries the Jews will carry with them the memory of a great wrong. They will carry it in their genes and in their subconscious, even in the unlikely event of universal brotherhood and amity. Just so, the Brehonys harboured their grudge over the centuries and the Sheehys looked at the hill and the good land around it and felt an ancestral grief.

Deep thoughts, these were, but in fact they took a long time to come together. Years later I sat in a pub and watched the Pope on the television news. He was standing in the Jordan and extending forgiveness to the Jews. I was struck by his lack of sensitivity, to say the least. Time was when we used to give the Jews a right old dressing-down on Good Friday. Maybe he offered to buy them all a drink and forget all about it. I had another bottle of stout and gave the matter some thought. Apparently the Jews did not show the appropriate gratitude.

More practical matters intruded. Exams were taken and I returned home. I got my old job back and assumed a watching brief. Badger had got the thatcher in to give the cottage a short back and sides. The thatch shone like gold. He went to the quarry and filled the back seat of the car with burnt lime. We watched it seething in buckets and turning miraculously into whitewash and then, with big distemper brushes, we attacked the walls, slapping on the dazzling whiteness and whistling as we worked. He was always in a good mood and liberal with both praise and a few bob.

I got a ladder to go up to the peak of the gable. In County Meath they wrap the thatch around a hipped roof but in our part of the world the chimney stood on top of the gable. There was one place where a stone appeared to be missing. Old layers of whitewash, like broken oystershell, surrounded the hole. I went down to find a stone to plug the gap but Badger told me to leave it alone.

"But won't the rain get in?" I protested. "I can fill it in and dab the whitewash over it. Why spoil the ship?"

"Yerrah, leave it," he said again. "It's always been like that." I shrugged, but it offended my sense of neatness. Badger shuffled and kicked at a pebble. He stood back and admired the work, squinting his eyes at the glare.

"Just finish the chimney," he said, "and we can call it a day."

"But why not do the job right?" I asked again, indicating the hole.

"Well, the way it is, since you won't leave go, it's an old custom that you never finish a house completely, in case you might annoy the gentry. It might be in their way, like."

"The landlords. Is that what you mean?"

"No, no, not them gentry. The other ones. The little fellas," and he nodded, I swear to God, in the direction of the hill.

"The fairies!" I burst out laughing.

"Aw, laugh away," he said grinning sheepishly. "It's only an old custom, but I'll not be the one to break it."

"Go 'way," I scoffed, "a grown man like you."

Badger sniffed and wiped the back of his hand across his nose.

"That's the story anyway," he said with an air of finality, "Take it or leave it. They used to say we only borrow the land. That's why we've no right to build anything too permanent."

I looked at the cottage. It seemed to grow out of the ground. It was probably centuries old, older than the haunted house.

"What about that other house then?" I asked and immediately regretted the question. What if he were to decide to take me over there? The key on the mantelpiece would not fit. Enquiries and finger prints would lead inevitably to me.

"Ah well, they say," he began, distancing himself to avoid ridicule, "they say it was built across a fairy-track if you must know. It never had any luck."

He looked across the yard towards the clump of dark pines and the old stone building, and shook his head. "There was never any luck in that house at all, at all."

"Why don't you knock it down, then?" I asked.

"God, you're an extraordinary fuckin' genius," he said in amusement. "You want answers for everything. When I was your age I knew enough words and had enough ideas to keep me goin' for a lifetime."

I felt rebuked.

"I know you're a great man for the readin' but there's some things it's better not to know. Leave the oul' house alone and the bad luck that's in it. That's what I say."

I thought about his views on the way home. 'Enough words' suggested a kind of security, a self-confidence that had no need of book-learning. I began to think of curiosity as a kind of affliction. It certainly proved fatal to the cat. Ideas could be very disturbing. It was interesting though, about the stone. It was a bit like the way we never unpacked our case at school, a fear of permanence. Still there was a lot of ignorance and superstition in what he said. In the final analysis wasn't it better to look into things. There was nothing in the haunted house but dust and jackdaws, nests and a bit of hysterical play-acting from Kate.

I became part of Badger's team when it came to putting up bales of straw for the motor-bike races. We took the tractor and trailer out in the evenings before the races and lagged lampposts and dangerous bends with barricades of straw. We marked rough spots on the road with whitewash, a hint to the county council road maintenance men, and we put up impressive hoardings with diagrams of the bends. I could go in and out of the pits as often as I wanted and spent a lot of time just hanging around observing the colourful pageant of last minute preparations. I gained some knowledge of technical terms as well as some colourful profanity to expand my vocabulary.

The Sheehy lads were as amiable as ever but I could not accuse Kate of going out of her way to talk to me. She was pleasant enough to Badger, still calling him Mr Brehony, which I found reassuring, but I noticed, hawklike, that she seemed to have a lot to say to John Olford from up the hill. It was not obvious to other people around, but whenever he was in the yard, she seemed to find an excuse to go down through the weeds to the washing line and stop for a word with him on the way back. Sometimes she picked through the jungle of raspberry canes and would stand talking to him and popping the berries one by one into her mouth. I saw her offering some to him and how he spread his oily hands as if declining, only to have her put the berries into his mouth. He laughed at something she said and resumed his tinkering.

I moved nearer, greeting her casually. She seemed irritated by the intrusion. The young man looked up at me without any particular interest. He was, I judged, in his middle twenties with what struck me as an air of off-hand self-confidence. A lock of hair fell across his forehead as he bent to his work. He brushed it back, leaving a dark oil streak on his brow. He looked very dashing and capable and I disliked him instantly.

He pushed the machine forward off the stand and worked the kick-start gently, sensing the compression. I ventured a knowledgeable remark, but my words were lost in the roar of the engine. Casually he twisted the throttle, blasting me into irrelevance.

“I want to give her a run,” he shouted over the noise, “so I can give you a lift if you like. Side-saddle though.”

“I have to go into town,” she said half-defensively. “I might as well take a lift.”

It seemed to me that she sat unnecessarily close to him on the racing saddle. Her skirt fluttered above her knees and she clutched at it ineffectually with one hand, while her other arm encircled his waist. At the gate he braked sharply and she was thrown against him. She gave me a little self-conscious wave, just a fluttering of fingers and was gone. The engine blared, derisively I thought, and I stood listening to the dwindling sound. I hope he breaks his stupid neck, I thought and the world felt cold and desolate all of a sudden. I kicked at a stone and decided to go home. Badger was standing some distance away. He still clutched the bale that he had been lifting but it was as if he had been frozen in the act of loading it onto the trailer. His features were distorted by an expression of pure hatred and I noticed even at a distance, that the tendons of his wrists and hands stood out like wire. He caught my eye and I recognised something in his glance. It was as if we were conspirators. I turned away quickly and wandered off. I remembered that look a long time afterwards.

I lost my taste for motor-cycling from that time onwards. On the day of the races I took the train to Dublin, feeling almost like a traitor. The crowds were already gathering on the railway bank. The hawkers and day trippers were alighting from the down trains, but the holiday mood could not penetrate my black depression.

I wandered around the city for the whole afternoon, looking in shop windows. I even went up Nelson’s Pillar. They had wisely put a cage over the catwalk or I might have been tempted to do an Eddie Heron onto the pavement below. I went into a news and cartoon cinema and failed to raise even a smile at the antics of Ollie and Stan. Nasser was going on about his country’s right to the Suez Canal.

I could picture my brothers arguing about the race. They thought I had gone mad and were very resentful of my whole attitude. To make matters worse they were looking forward to the dance after the race, where the prizes would be presented. All the riders would be there. I could just imagine them. Kate, of course would be there too, queening it over everyone, no doubt. To hell with the lot of them.

I contemplated going away for good but I was getting hungry and had only a few bob in my pocket. There was no future in that. I went home. My mother put food in front of me and my father raised his eyebrows, eloquently signalling to her to say nothing. There were grilled tomatoes, pigs' kidneys, lambs' liver, fried eggs, rashers, sausages and fried onion rings. I postponed thoughts of suicide for the time being and decided to soldier on.

In the middle of the night I heard Fergal and Anto coming in from the dance. They were horsing about and laughing while making a pretence of trying to be quiet. They were not drunk but, as they say, they had drink taken. This would cause serious problems if they woke the parents. I went downstairs to forestall them and I must admit, to glean whatever information I could. I gathered that it had been a great night. Olford had got the fastest lap prize. He had been brilliant. Badger had got langers and had to be asked to leave. They had had a few themselves. Olford had addressed him as Badger and he had taken exception. There had not really been a fight but it could have come to it.

"I think it was John Wahab started it," snorted Fergal.

"Who?" I asked puzzled.

This occasioned more laughter.

"Olford," laughed Anto. "John Wahab Olford. There's a name for you. He called him 'Badger', to his face."

"I never knew that," I admitted. "That's a funny name."

"They had an argument about shooting. Badger said if he caught him shooting over the marsh he'd break his bloody neck." Anto guffawed. "He said Olford couldn't shoot for nuts. He said he couldn't hit a cow on the arse with a plank. He was in a fierce mood."

"What did your man say?" I asked, fascinated. I knew what lay behind this of course, but I was saying nothing.

"He just said, kind of superior like, 'Cool down Badger, old man,' and went to walk away." Fergal mimicked Olford's rather supercilious tone.

"Yeah," agreed Anto, "that really got him goin'. 'Old man,' says he, 'I'll show him who's an old man, be Jaysus.' He was nearly foamin' at the mouth. Your man just ignored him after that and they had to get Badger to leave. It was gas, really."

I questioned them further but made no mention of Kate. I knew that she was the cause of the trouble and inwardly I was sorry that Badger had come out so badly. We shared, I thought, a common rejection. We were fellows in adversity and I could find a small corner of my misery where I could pity him, now that he was no longer a rival.

Ten

I have a talent for getting the wrong end of the stick. Badger had not given up hope as it transpired. He was still pressing his suit, as could be seen on Sunday mornings. Sometimes he wore a very natty sports jacket and flannels and suede shoes were observed once or twice. Dan Sheehy still had use of the Volkswagen whenever he wanted it and they seemed to be on very good terms. I even saw him at a distance, talking to Kate. She had apparently got very quiet and morose. She still went up to the hill occasionally but I had given up going there. There was no point in it. I did not want to meet her although I wanted to see her and know what she was doing. I developed a kind of sixth sense about her and could tell when she was in the vicinity and always felt a tremor of fear at the thought of having to talk to her. My sense of failure built up a kind of resentment.

Badger put me to sorting seed potatoes into boxes. I had to stack the boxes in a loft over the shed where he kept the tractor. I worked away by myself, whistling softly and looked forward to my lunch. A little light came in through the half open door and the trapdoor from below. It was pleasant to work at my own pace. The loft smelt of earth, like a cave.

I sat down on an upturned box and opened my sandwiches, savouring the moment of anticipation before the first bite. The trapdoor was diminished to a thin slit of light, through which I could see part of the doorway below. There was a spattering of rain on the tiles above me. I heard a soft foot-fall below in the shed and was aware of Kate stepping in out of the rain.

I froze in the act of biting into the sandwich. I knew there were onions in it. The crunch would surely betray my presence. I could watch her for a while and then perhaps make my presence known. Onions would be a deadener on conversation. She leaned her head against the door-jam and looked up. For a moment I was sure that she would see me staring down at her. I need not have feared. She looked tired and worried and I immediately repented of the harsh things I had thought about her. I was on the point of making a noise when the door was darkened by another figure. It was Badger of course, and he did not seem a bit surprised to find her there.

I looked around for some means of escape. The loft door was a good ten feet off the ground. I could make noise with the boxes, but something impelled me to keep quiet. Somehow, I had to know the worst.

"Have ye been thinkin' about what I said?" began Badger without preamble. She turned her head away.

"I had a word with the Daddy," he said more gently.

"It's no skin off his nose," she replied with, I thought, a touch of defiance.

"Yerra now, he's a reasonable man and so am I. I've made a fair offer. Fair and square."

He put his right hand on the door jamb on a level with her head, as if to block her avenue of retreat.

For what seemed a long time there was silence between them. I could see that she was trying to speak, but the words seemed to dry up in her throat.

"You're a fine sturdy young woman," he began again, "but ye won't get many better offers than mine. Any money that comes with ye, ye can keep for yourself. What do you say to that now?"

Suave, I thought contemptuously. How could any woman resist such blandishments? I waited for her dismissive response, perhaps even incredulous laughter.

"And the hill will be mine?" she asked quietly, looking directly at him for the first time.

"All signed and sealed," he nodded, "as soon as the knot is tied."

"Mine and nobody else's?" she insisted. "Nobody's to plough or to burn or anything?"

"All yours," he agreed and there was a shake in his voice.

"All right then," she almost mumbled, but I thought I saw a flicker of a smile, a quick grin of triumph.

He went to embrace her but she twisted out of his grasp.

"Be God, girl, I could pour at ye now," he groaned and his voice was slurred. I felt my stomach turning. She gave a short dry laugh and moved out of my line of vision, out into the rain.

"None of that now," she said almost teasingly. I heard retreating footsteps. Badger punched a fist into the palm of his hand several times. He gave a little laugh. "Be the powers!" he muttered several times to himself in obvious glee. "Be the powers o' war."

The wave of nausea passed and I heard him rattling at the tractor. Occasionally he chuckled aloud. After a few minutes the engine rattled into life and the building reverberated to the sound. Blue exhaust fumes rose through the trapdoor. I took a bite of the sandwich which had all the time been clutched in my fingers. It tasted of clay, of cobwebs and of T.V.O.

I waited a while and then made my escape by the upper door, dropping to the ground and hurrying away. By way of disguise I filled two buckets of water at the pump and took them around to the cottage. The old woman glowered at me.

"I didn't ask for water," she grumbled. She had the fire irons in her hand, a poker and tongs, and in amazement I watched as she placed them on the doorstep in the form of a cross.

"That strap will not enter this house while I'm alive," she said, not addressing me in particular. "That fool won't give everything away, if I can help it."

With that the tractor stopped outside and Badger stepped in the door almost tripping over the irons. He sent them scattering with a kick.

"What in the name of Jaysus?" he expostulated and laughed, "Nearly broke me snitch."

I wish you would, I reflected silently.

He rubbed his hands, in great good humour.

"I'm off into town," he said jovially. "I've an odious thirst on me." I headed for the door and he called after me, "Don't forget to finish that seed now."

"Oh," I lied airily, "I finished that hours ago."

"Heh," he laughed, "takin' it easy then, were ye? Howan'ever there's plenty for ye to do while I'm away."

He rubbed his hands again "Good lad, good lad" he went on, beaming on me, as he climbed onto the seat of the tractor. "Tell the oul' woman I'll be back roarin' for me tea in a couple of hours."

"Tell her yourself," I muttered as he disappeared in an azure cloud. "I'm not hangin' around here to be humiliated."

I looked around the yard cultivating a strong sense of grievance. The sound of the tractor faded. I realised that I was getting wet. I was glad that Dan Sheehy had his car. I hoped that he would be soaked. He had no overcoat on and had omitted even the traditional sack over the shoulders. I was surrounded by an oppressive silence. From far away I heard the throb of a motor cycle engine. Reluctantly I turned towards the seed loft and unfinished work. That would be an end of my career as a farmer I decided.

I had to take evasive action after that. I made excuses for a few days and finally hit on the right formula. I declared myself to be fed-up working. Being fed-up is almost a clinical condition and it covers a multitude. Adults assume that it will pass inevitably, but I think it should be officially recognised. Dr. So and So is ceasing practice at such and such an address because he is fed-up with patients complaining about their insides. Her Majesty has dissolved Parliament because she is fed-up listening to arguments and evasions. Cromwell did something like that, did he not?

I succeeded in avoiding Badger for most of the following week, but early one morning the tractor and trailer arrived at the station just as I was coming out of the house. I was nabbed.

"I didn't see ye over beyond," he said, closing the throttle. The silence precluded any escape. He stirred his cap and scratched his head interrogatively.

"Ah no," I began lamely. "I wasn't feelin' too spry. Thought I ought to give it a rest for a while."

"Aye. Do ye tell me so?" He swung down out of the seat. "Well sure, maybe ye'd give me a hand for a few minutes. I have to collect a yoke off the train. It should be on the far platform."

"Sure," I said expansively. "No bother."

My father beckoned from across the tracks. He was leaning on a small upright bogie. Beside him lay the components of an enormous double bed, lately unloaded from the Dublin train. Even at a distance I could see a kind of a smirk on his face.

"That's a hell of a farrowin' crate," he observed as we came up the steps from the tunnel.

"Heh," Badger laughed, obviously feeling very self-conscious. "Be God it's bigger than I thought."

I felt a surge of hatred, picturing himself and his young wife threshing about on the bed, which would still incongruously be wrapped in its protective brown paper and string. And he expected me to help him carry it. Still there was no escape. We made three trips of it, across the barrow-path with the sections balanced athwart the little bogie. The mattress seemed to have a life of its own. It struggled out of our grasp and tried to escape when we were heaving it onto the trailer. Eventually the task was finished and away he went.

My father went up into the signal box. He made some remark to the signalman. Their heads went back in silent guffaws inside the glass cage. I could see very little to laugh about. Now that I knew the score I could see that *el Gavilan* was getting nowhere. The morning we mitched from school came suddenly to my mind. There was a kestrel, a witch, motionless in the sky. I remembered how it slanted suddenly, spilling the wind and hurtling downwards behind the hill. It was time for me to make some move before it was too late.

I met her coming out of the cinema by herself. My sixth sense had let me down. I had sat through J.A. Fitzpatrick, a cartoon, Movietone and a very irritating musical, without realising that she was only a couple of rows behind me. In the film assorted young women broke into song and dance at improbable moments, while being ardently pursued by middle-aged men in double-breasted suits. Moustaches and hair-oil were much in evidence, on the men that is, but true love triumphed in the end and the heroine renounced a Broadway career to go back to the boy she had first loved. There was much relief all round and a deal of singing and dancing. I remained glued to my seat throughout, not so much from a love of romance, as from the deposits of discarded chewing-gum that adorned the arms of the chair and the floor beneath. All the same I thought, if only life could be like that. I am however an indifferent singer. I draw a discreet veil across the subject of my dancing. I digress.

"Hello," I said, adopting the direct approach.

"Oh hello," she replied without any obvious enthusiasm.

"Walk along with you," I offered, not making it a question, for fear of a refusal.

"Sure," she said, wrapping her arms across her bosom and holding her elbows. She shivered. There was an autumnal chill in the air. The darkness, I thought, made for a certain intimacy, the anonymity of the confessional.

"You'll be back to school soon, I suppose," she ventured.

"Shades of the prison house," I agreed.

"What? Oh yes. I see what you mean."

We walked for a time in silence.

"What about yourself?"

"Oh, probably commercial college or something like that."

"What about Badger then?" I had said it. It was out. My life hung by a thread.

"Badger?" Her voice was high-pitched, wary.

"Yes. Aren't you going to marry him?"

She walked along, hugging herself and looking at the ground.

"It's not as simple as all that."

"Everyone says you are," I pressed.

"Everyone can mind their own business."

"Including me?" She looked sideways at me and hesitated.

"It's just not as simple as everyone thinks."

I said nothing, biding my time. There was a glimmer of hope still.

"We'll just have to wait and see."

We walked in silence. I kicked at the little drifts of sand that had blown up from the beach. I tried out some gambits in my head. I declared undying devotion a couple of times but, no matter how I phrased it, it sounded mawkish and juvenile. I had no land to offer her. I could not even offer her a lift home. That was it.

"It's your man, isn't it?"

"Who?"

"John Wahab Olford," I loaded the name with subtle contempt. I knew I had her then. She shivered again.

"You're very shrewd, aren't you?"

"Fairly shrewd," I agreed.

"Have you been spying on me, or what?"

"Didn't have to," I said, grateful for the darkness. "So what are you going to do?" I could have said that I did not think much of her taste, either way.

"Well, if it's any of your business, I just don't know."

"If you marry Badger you'll own the land," I said slyly.

Again, she looked at me sharply. I stared straight ahead.

"What do you know about that?"

"Stands to reason, doesn't it?"

"Yes, I suppose so. Land isn't everything though."

"No, that's true." Perhaps I was inserting a little wedge of uncertainty in her mind.

We went on through the town, not speaking for a long while until we came to the railway arch.

"I'll go along with you," I offered. "I'm in no rush home."

We were in the country now, away from the street lights. The darkness was almost palpable. A thin sliver of moon hung low over the western horizon.

"Do you ever get nervous walking out here by yourself?" I queried, for want of something better to say.

"What is there to be afraid of? I'm well used to it."

There were low stirrings in the hedgerows on either side.

"It's strange to think of all the little creatures that live all around us and we never see them. Isn't it?" I remarked.

"I suppose people walk on them and never even notice," she agreed. "We think we're the only important things on this earth."

She stopped suddenly and gripped my arm. "Look," she said pointing upwards, "a shooting star. Make a wish."

A phosphorescent speck swam for an instant across the black immensity of the sky and was gone. I felt her hand still on my arm and I wished silently and fervently.

"There's another," she said excitedly.

"Meteorites," I said unable to resist the urge to explain. "They always come at this time of year."

"I might have known you'd know all about them," she laughed and tucked her hand under my arm. We strolled on like, I imagined, an old married couple.

"What else did the book say?"

"It wasn't a book actually. It was a magazine. They're called the Perseids and they come around every year."

"Is that so?" She stumbled slightly and bumped against me.

"They used to be called the Tears of St. Laurence," I added. "He was some early martyr."

"Not our fellow, then?"

"No."

"The Tears of St. Laurence. I like that."

We had come to the top of the rise and to our right was the ragged black outline of the wood and the very top of Brehonys' Hill showing darkly behind it.

"Maybe they fell on the hill," she said quietly, "the tears."

I said nothing, conscious of her closeness.

"Whatever happens, will you still be my friend?" she asked suddenly.

"Of course," I replied. She sounded a bit melodramatic.

"I think you understand things more than most people."

"Tell you the truth, I'm nuts about you myself. If you don't —." It was not exactly how I had intended broaching the matter.

She stopped me with a finger on my lips.

"Not a word now," she said. "I can't explain everything just yet." She put her hand into the pocket of her skirt. "Look, you mind this for me. Whenever I ask for it back I'll tell you the whole story — when you're a bit older."

I put out my hand and felt a smooth round stone. It was warm from her pocket.

"Just a memento," she said. "It might bring you luck."

I had hoped for more, a secret or a confidence or even a chance to touch her again and was disappointed.

"I promise I'll explain everything sometime," she said again. "I must go in now."

There was a light on in the kitchen of her house. She faded away from me and presently I saw her silhouette passing the lighted window. I felt the warmth of the stone in my hand. More of her play-acting I deduced but something prompted me not to throw it away.

When I studied it at home under the light I recognised it as the stone she had picked up at the old house the day she alleged that she burned her hands on the bar. I could see the speckles of gold under the smooth surface. Perhaps they were imprisoned grains of meteorite waiting to be released. I put it away in a drawer and lay on my bed thinking about her. I should have been more forceful and, with a fair following wind, she might have yielded to me, not a stone, but her soft and lissom body. I cursed myself not for the first time, for an inarticulate oaf. If your brother asks of you an egg, do you reach him a stone? With my luck, yes. Or was it a scorpion?

I fell asleep in my clothes and dreamed the most confusing dreams of a startlingly erotic nature. I woke up wondering if I was in some way to blame. Was it matter for confession? It was not intentional, but I had enjoyed it.

In a couple of weeks I was back in school, not having seen her again. We all seemed a lot bigger and older after the summer and occasionally I noted with satisfaction, I needed a shave. A classmate sold me an old cut-throat razor that was guaranteed to save a fortune in blades, a dangerous looking thing, German steel. Unfortunately I pared a pencil with it and took a large bight out of the blade and had to revert to Mac's Smile with the reversible smiling face on the packet.

It felt good to be shaving and no longer to be the little brother. Fergal and Anto had passed on to higher things and had become only a faint memory to their teachers. Occasionally their names were invoked as an example to me, but when I looked in the mirror and scraped at the emerging fuzz, I saw a strong determined face. I was my own man, a man who could look life in the face and bear the scars. In fact I bore a good many scars until I got the hang of shaving. For a while I looked like a case of failed hara-kiri. It was probably a good thing that the cut-throat was put out of commission.

There was a lot of blood around in those days, at least metaphorically speaking. One of my classmates was haemophiliac and suffered a great deal from bleeding into his joints. He also bruised very easily and a tooth extraction required his removal to hospital. I wondered how he could live with the knowledge that, at any time, a minor slip could be the end of him. I imagined a cataract of blood gushing from the smallest scratch. I tended to speak very gently to him for fear of jarring his mechanism, but in between crises, he was as cheerful a soul as you could meet.

It seemed to be accepted without question in our history texts, that shedding blood, one's own or anyone else's, was unequivocally a good thing for one's country. Our history was written in the blood of martyrs. Patriots called for blood sacrifice and the earth was warmed with blood, shed generously and without remorse. Blood dripped from holy pictures and the whole iconography became confused, interchanging patriot with saint and vice versa. Wolfe Tone, a staunch Protestant, sat uneasily amid all the devotion. Pearse revelled in it and assiduously sought his own Calvary. Those who survived to old age, who cobbled things together to enable people to go on living, were relegated to footnotes and obscurity. Martyrs held the centre of the stage. I wondered if, wherever they were, they knew what had been achieved and whether they drew a ghostly satisfaction from parades, flag-waving and memorial plaques. Somehow I doubted it and resolved to go easy on the blood.

In later years there was a great vogue for songs about blood letting, usually accompanied by great consumption of beer, but gradually the vultures came home to roost. The icons were reversed and people saw the reality of families spattered on the streets by random bombing and the bullet-riddled corpse lying by the side of a country road. I still think of Mr O'Meara's theory about the primeval forest and the dark places that lurk in the corners of the human mind and as yet, I have not come to terms with the elation I felt when I first heard about the murder.

Eleven

It was always referred to as the murder. A bad business, my father wrote. Badger's gun was taken for forensic tests. What that might prove, I could not imagine. He used the thing all year round on vermin and game, in due season. Even his snares were taken for examination. He wrote discreetly, making no accusation, but I had a picture of my old friend creeping up behind his victim in the woods and garrotting him in the dead of night. I felt a surge of guilty relief. Olford was dead and Badger was surely out of the running. But what of Kate?

My father mentioned a very delicate matter. Kate Sheehy had gone away. It was rumoured that she was going to have a baby. He made no suggestion as to who the father, the guilty party, might have been and, for one mad moment, I wondered if he suspected me. That was absurd. He said that he wanted to tell me as gently as possible, as he knew I was friendly with the individuals involved and might be asked to give evidence at some stage. I blanched at the thought that I might have to admit to eavesdropping. I might be seen as some kind of accessory. My hands were clean.

I crumpled the letter in my fist and stared unseeing at the wall. Rorschach blots blossomed in my field of vision. A baby! That meant — it was unthinkable. He deserved what he got, the bastard. Of course, to a Protestant it was not such a great sin in itself, but he had led an innocent girl astray. My mother, I reflected later, probably saw it the other way around, all her old suspicions confirmed. I was glad he was dead.

I wrote home immediately for further news. Badger had often been heard uttering threats against the young man. After the disappearance of the unfortunate young man, suspicions had been aroused and enquiries had been made. Badger had been interviewed by the Guards, as my father put it. He had not quite reached the stage of helping the police with their enquiries. I was given to understand that the Guards had been all over the farm and the woods for days but, as yet, nothing incriminating had been found. Badger had not been arrested, although people were avoiding him. He was protesting his innocence of any wrong-doing in such a truculent way as to make his own case worse.

The evidence such as it was, was highly circumstantial. Intuitively however, I knew where the body was hidden. I remembered Badger's remark about caves under the hill. I knew with a fierce certainty, that in some ancient chamber under the old fort, the body of John Wahab Olford was hidden away. I could see him crouched in the foetal position in some ancient cist, like the black skeletons in the museum reconstructions. His motor-cycle which had also disappeared, was undoubtedly sunk somewhere in the swamp. With a mine detector I could have located it for them, but I saw no reason why I should. It was enough to know that I could solve the whole business if I wanted to. However I still owed something to Badger. The trail had gone cold. It was not up to me to put the hounds onto an old friend. The thought made me feel quite virtuous.

In this country there is a saint for almost every townland. It seems as if a lifetime of living alone in want and squalor and occasionally cursing the neighbours, was enough to qualify for sanctity by popular acclaim. No Devil's Advocate was needed to rake over the local traditions. It was enough for the faithful that he had opened the earth to swallow an impious farmer on the sabbath or had chased people off their island home with his amazing expanding cloak.

Saint Laurence, who eventually made it officially, prayed against an officer who had killed his servant. The man fell and broke his leg which went gangrenous. He died satisfactorily in terrible agony. Badger likewise, became a murderer by popular acclaim. He was eventually taken in for questioning which is as good as guilty to all fair-minded observers, but nothing was found. No oil stains leaked up to betray the presence of an incriminating machine. No corpse was located. They could pin nothing on Badger.

The file, that terrifying vortex into which every chance remark and bizarre coincidence is swept, remained open. People were free to speculate and make assertions, and, in a guilty parenthesis, to feel that John Olford was not, after all, one of ours. His doom had been assured centuries ago through ancestral guilt. But most of all, it was good to be alive, to blame and excuse, to justify or shake the head and say it was a very bad business indeed.

At Christmas I was able to make fuller enquiries. The excitement had died down. We did not go up to Olford Hall for holly. Some fellow came around with a lorry selling Christmas trees and holly, so that removed the necessity. Just as animals abandon an injured companion people drew back from encountering the old man. I did venture across the fields in the direction of the hill, hoping that I would not meet Badger along the way. It would be hard to know what to say. 'Find any bodies lately?' would not be very appropriate. The reeds and rushes formed small islands in the flooded swamp, an ideal place to lose something. In the films there is always an incriminating piece of evidence, the vital clue that wraps the whole thing up. I saw no clues, but then again I needed none. I knew the whole story already.

From a distance I could see a car outside Badger's cottage. Most likely Dublin Castle had sent some heavies down to grill poor Badger. I hoped he could stick to his story, whatever it might be. I knew the law was relentless and would stay on the trail forever, if necessary.

Afterwards I learned that the doctor had been called to the old woman but that it was too late. She was buried after Christmas on a day when the east wind blew straight out of Siberia, a wind guaranteed to carry off a couple of the mourners, if they could be described as such. In fact, I think, most people came along out of curiosity, in some degree to marvel at the size of the coffin but mainly to have a good look at Badger. It was not every day that you got a chance to see a real murderer face to face and even to shake his hand. There was, I would say, a fair measure of sympathy for him, but nonetheless he was something of an embarrassment. While not wishing him any harm, it would have been better all round if they had taken him away and hanged him. In that way the business could have been sorted out properly in people's minds and argued back and forth until it fell into its proper perspective.

Badger had deteriorated. The suit had got a bit shabby and it looked as if he had forgotten to put in his collar bones.

"He looks a big shagged," muttered an old man to his companion.

"Gone downhill," agreed the other loudly. I knew him to be hard of hearing. He spoke loudly and heads turned.

"Hard on him, all the same," he continued in a stage whisper.

"Aye," nodded the first speaker. "Didn't deserve all this trouble." They nodded sympathetically in agreement.

"Wasn't his fault," said the deaf man again. "Didn't deserve all this trouble." He spoke with a hand in front of his mouth.

The other man nodded, aware that their conversation was carrying. I found myself watching them. They wore long black overcoats on which the dandruff lodged conspicuously. One carried a tweed cap with the front stud open, while the other turned his hat in his hands. The band was stained with hairoil. These were men whose opinions were valued, unofficial chroniclers of the town.

"Fucker got what he deserved if you ask me," averred the deaf man. "Nine hundred years of it," he added significantly. This time there were grins and nudges in the immediate neighbourhood.

"Poor oul' Dan Sheehy," sighed the first speaker, the sadness of it all making his voice tremble, "badly let down by that young one of his."

Dan was standing close by the grave and at that moment he reached over to shake Badger by the hand. The onlookers relished the moment, each one putting his or her interpretation on the episode. I must admit that I wondered what was going through their minds at that time.

"No better than she should be," confided the deaf man to all and sundry. Somebody shushed him and he took the hint. I suspected that he used his deafness as a licence to say aloud what others might merely whisper. I could see how gradually the blame would surely settle on my poor Kate and how everyone would experience that warm feeling of fellowship, as they united in common cause to pick her to death and scatter her reputation to the four winds. I pushed my way through the throng and left them to it.

My father, strangely for him, saw no humour in the situation. I often caught him looking at me as if about to ask me some question. My mother's attitude was one of tenuous family loyalty to Badger.

"If he did do something, and mind you, I don't say that he did, then he was driven to it. The less said about it the better." So saying she would seal her lips in an expression of disapproval and the subject, for the time being, was closed.

Kate's brothers avoided me, turning their heads away and conversing among themselves when they saw me coming. I assumed that they had no wish to talk to anyone at all. I could get no information about her. It was as if she had vanished off the face of the earth.

Only Anto suggested that she had, as he said, gone to a home for bad ladies. We came to blows and unlike the stories where right triumphs over evil I came off worst. The violence made me feel better and when he had got over his surprise he was genuinely sorry.

"I didn't mean any harm," he said sheepishly. "It's just what I heard." I held a handkerchief to my bleeding nose.

"Fuck off," I said "and fuck the whole bloody lot of you. I'll be glad to get back to school out of this kip." He retreated, looking hurt and left me tilting my head back, trying to stop the blood. A key, I thought. That was what was usually used in such circumstances. That reminded me of something else they were saying; that Badger refused to give the police the key to the old house; that he tried to palm off a different key. They had to break down the door. Despite the fact that he said it had been locked for years there had been definite signs that someone had been in there not too long before. Here was the kind of clue that detectives delighted in. They had pulled up all the floorboards but nothing had, as yet, been found. Badger was a slippery customer all right.

I snuffled at the blood and dabbed away until the flow stopped. What if someone found the key in my possession? It would be a tricky one to explain. But I had, on the face of it, a fool-proof alibi. Still it would be no harm to get rid of it as soon as possible. I fished it out of my case and wiped off any possible fingerprints. Craftily I flicked it into the tender of the Belfast express when it made its regular halt. Somewhere between Dundalk and Newry, I guess, it went into the firebox of the Enterprise and was rapidly reduced to clinker. I was glad to get back to school, away from atmospheres and unfinished conversations.

For a time I believe my father thought that Badger would revert to being what he had been before, a kind of butt for a bit of gentle ribbing. His appearance certainly reverted to what it had been, but the drink took a hold on him. As far as I could gather he was never charged with anything, but the file, as they say, remained open. Sometimes he became maudlin, wanting to buy drink for his old friends, which included everyone within reach and then again, he became truculent, challenging anyone who caught his eye.

My mother said that he was killing himself.

"He's not the fill of his trousers," she asserted, which puzzled me at first. Then I had a look and right enough, the seat of his pants hung in folds and pleats 'a dead give-away', as she put it. He was definitely getting very scrawny.

I had the opportunity to observe him at regular intervals during school holidays and it came as a shock every time to see the damage he was doing to himself. He still went to mass and occupied his traditional seat. He became a sort of a lone bird. He looked neglected and my heart went out to him, but there was no way in which I could renew our former familiarity. My father, I noticed, had begun to refer to him in the past tense. He told the occasional story affectionately, but as if remembering an old friend — like when the L.D.F. was on manoeuvres during the war and set up their bivouacs on Brehonys' Bottoms. "Apparently some of the men complained about the size of the eggs they got for breakfast. This mind you, at a time of rationing, when people in England would be glad of a cup of tea. Indeed I remember the way we used to swap the coupons . . ."

"The eggs," I interrupted impatiently. He could be very irritating at times.

"Ah yes. Well, the complaint went to the cook and the cook took it to the quarter-master who sent for Badger. 'What's the meaning of this?' says the quarter-master and he holds up what looks like a pigeon's egg. We understood that you could supply us with decent sized eggs.' Well, Badger takes the egg there and then and off he goes down to the yard to tackle the hens."

I shuffled my feet. He took his time about getting to the point.

"It seems the hens appointed a spokesman, or spokeswoman, I suppose I should say. Whatever. Badger shows her the egg and demands an explanation. The hen looks him in the eye and says she: 'We've laid eggs for the British Army and we've laid eggs for the Irish army, but we're fucked if we'll burst our boilers layin' eggs for the Emergency army.'" He smiled as if in reminiscence. There must have been a time when that story produced guffaws at the expense of the L.D.F. members present, but I could see little point to it. The best of

Badger seemed to lie away back in the War years.

My father was rather like half of a comedy duo, the wiseacre without his straight man. He still enjoyed the radio but could make no sense of surrealist comedy like The Goons. 'Not those bloody Goons again, is it?' he would groan and then sit frowning and grumbling through thirty minutes of inspired lunacy, while the rest of us rolled around in glee. Whenever I hear the weather forecast I still hear The Famous Eccles saying 'winds light to variable', though why that should be funny is difficult to explain. Middle-aged men betray their age even yet, by breaking into Bluebottle and Seagoon voices when logic and reason fail to deal with a situation.

Badger gradually gave up driving the car. To be honest, he lost his licence when the Guards got fed up driving him home. In those days the drunken driver was regarded as a bit of a wag until the inevitable happened and someone got killed. The Guards rarely see the funny side of these things though.

One of the workmen had to take over driving the tractor to the market and gradually Badger began to let slip control of his affairs. Like his mode of dress the land began to show signs of neglect. The yellow weeds blossomed unchecked in the pastures and gradually Dan Sheehy's bit of land began to bear favourable comparison with that of his neighbour. Various explanations were advanced for the change. A broken heart. This one usually raised a bit of a laugh or at least, a pitying smile. 'There's no fool like an old fool. His mother used to say it would end in tears. He didn't deserve better. Didn't he get his chance when the first wife died?'

The bad luck was let out when they broke open the haunted house. Indeed the door still hung open but nobody was inclined to go in. Dark deeds was done there in the death of night — a nice alliterative phrase that gave the assertion the stamp of truth. Not for all the tea in China would the speaker spend the night in that house.

It might, of course, have been the gentry. This was always suggested with a theatrical lowering of the voice and a careful look around. 'Maybe they just got fed up and decided to take back the land. It's an old tradition around here y'know. Not that I put much pass on it meself, but ye never know.' There were opportunities here for some ham-acting, a touch of Barry Fitzgerald.

Guilt, of course was the obvious explanation that nobody liked to mention too openly. Judge not, that you be not sued. 'Remarks like that are actionable, but isn't it well known that murder will out? I mean, you can't go around with things like that on your conscience. And speaking of guilt, there were others involved too. Do you know that the nuns did everything for that girl; looked after her all the time she was expecting. Put their hands under her feet, they did and even got people to take the baby. And do you know, she wouldn't let the poor thing go. Refused point-blank to sign it over. There was a terrible scene, I believe, and those poor people downstairs, waiting to give the child a good home. I mean to say! Now I'm not sayin' anything that hasn't been said before and God knows I wouldn't wish any harm to a Christian, but that young man was too smart by half. He should have kept to his own kind and all this trouble would never have happened. Sure, God be good to him, wherever he is, lyin' out there without a prayer said over him. That land never had luck. Anyway, she won't show her face around here in a hurry.'

This was the received opinion, the orthodox view of what was generally accepted as a very bad business indeed. Time dulled the edges of the story until it could be told again among those who knew, merely by the raising of an eyebrow or the clicking of a tongue when Badger toppled his glass on the bar counter or glared around him with red and rheumy eyes, challenging the company to accuse him to his face.

I graduated to having a drink when I started University. Pubs were still pubs in those days, where men congregated to discuss matters of moment over a drink, without being assaulted by canned music or drunken adolescents. I put up my hours on bottles of stout and, by and large, kept my opinions to myself when my elders were speaking. They saw Badger as the man who had cheated the hangman only to do the job himself. 'Mr Pierpoint will make no money outa' Badger', it was said. It was a gruesome joke, but there was a horrible truth to it.

As often as not Dan Sheehy got him home, which was only fair as Dan had acquired the Volkswagen. It had got more low-slung over the years and the exhaust pipe depended on a loop of bull-wire, or rather the end of the pipe, for the silencer had given up the ghost a long time ago. She sounded more like a fishing-boat as she chugged up the street. The spark had gone out of Dan too. They said that he was buttering Badger up in the hopes of getting the land, but those in the know scoffed at this, saying that the bank owned the place and was only waiting for a chance to sell it out from under him.

Twelve

In the margin of a map there is a diagram showing the magnetic variation. Mr O'Meara had explained its meaning, the nub of which is that not even the magnetic pole is constant. In your navigation you must allow for the fact that the pole itself is wandering. Your compass will follow the pole but the pole reserves the right to slip away from its appointed place on the map and mooch about the top of the world. During those few years I felt as if my lode star had shifted. The maps were in order. I was gainfully employed as a student of architecture. I was aiming at a degree and a decent job and I gave satisfaction all the way. I loved the business of plans and diagrams and the language of architecture. I dreamed of throwing up great structures of spindly steel and glass to catch the light and reflect the drifting clouds. People would crane their necks back to look up at these gleaming towers and would see in them the hand of the master. I saw cities stretching up into the blue, hanging gardens immune from the rigours of the Irish climate and environments designed for people to live an orderly and serene existence, safe from wind and rain.

But in a corner of my heart it was always raining, a grey, driving rain of the sort that dislodges clay from the sides of slopes and carries the soil away in yellow scummy torrents. I could not see clearly for the drifting veils of rain, but in there somewhere was a place and a time that was lost.

I never built the cities in the sky except on paper and as models. Though I say it myself, I excelled at making models. In a way, the vision was enough for me, the glimpse of what might have been. Someone else could take my idea and run with it and good luck to them. It has always given me intense pleasure to visit a site and see the building rising out of the confusion, while feeling glad at the same time that I was not carrying blocks or sawing timber. I love the smell of fresh plaster and the icy breeze that whistles through unglazed windows. It gives me a thrill to see roof timbers go up, leaning on the purlin, the purlin lounging on its struts and the whole thing staying up because, paradoxically, everything is falling into place. The flag goes up with the roof tree and everyone repairs to the pub.

Of course most of my work has been more mundane, down to earth and profitable. A builder takes my blueprint and rolls out two hundred identical houses. I show him how he can get forty-eight houses into a site instead of forty-seven and he is suitably grateful. Dublin sprawled outwards and my fortunes expanded with it.

My brother Anto marked the passing of time. He married and settled down in the town. He had the makings of the stereotyped frustrated civil servant, railing constantly against the system which contributed to his weal and that of his rapidly growing brood.

"I must be growing old," he remarked to me sadly one day.

"Why do you say that?"

"I bought some timber yesterday, to do a job in the house."

"So?"

"Time was I would have purloined it."

Ah, I thought, how the mighty have fallen, when a man like my brother is reduced to sordid commerce. Purloin a purlin. He never lost his sense of humour, although his economics were a mystery to me. I liked Jean, his wife. He was very lucky to find her. Not many would have put up with his fecklessness. Fergal was in the bank down the country. He rose rapidly through the ranks and assumed a serious mien. When I looked at the pair of them I thought of the Reverend Sydney Smith's remark when asked why his brother, a notable poltroon, had risen to be a peer of the realm. 'Gravity,' he said, 'raised him up, while levity drew me down.' Fergal wore a waistcoat which was beginning to stretch while Anto was engaged in a perpetual struggle with the wolf-pack at the door.

I got a flat in Dublin for the winter months but it suited me fine to spend the summers at home. One night when I came in off the late train Badger was sitting in the kitchen. I gathered that he had fallen in the gate and hit his head on a stone. He sat slumped in a chair gazing at a mug of soup that my mother had heated for him. It was cooling rapidly, as could be seen from the globules of fat that were gathering at the surface. There was a sticky-plaster on his forehead and a smear of blood on the side of his face. He looked a wreck. My mother offered him a bed for the night.

"We've plenty of room nowadays," she assured him.

"You might as well take it easy," added my father offhand, as if an idea had just occurred to him. He could have said 'you are drunk and incapable and a danger to yourself, if not to others', but that would not have been mannerly. There is a protocol in dealing with drunks and the last thing you must mention is the fact that he has taken too much alcohol. You could hint at the possibility that he was not himself, in a way shifting any blame, but to offer unsolicited help is tantamount to an insult.

"Ah no, Tom, I'm grand," he mumbled. "Just give me time to get me breath." He wheezed for a minute or so and took a tentative drag at the soup before putting it aside.

"It's no trouble," my father assured him, looking at me for corroboration. I noticed how my parents had gradually begun to turn to me for reassurance, a kind of imprimatur. I was supposed to be the one with the brains and the education. There was even a note of deference at times.

I had no solution to offer. We had no car and the station was deserted. There was no one who could be button-holed for a lift. I suggested ringing for a taxi but Badger roused himself to dismiss the idea as outrageous. Why part with good money when he could cut across the fields? So he would not stay and neither could he go.

He dozed for a little while and teetered on the chair. I caught him before he could fall. He hooked his finger into the handle of the mug and drew it towards him. We watched helplessly as the mug wobbled every time he swayed, until my mother, with great presence of mind, confiscated it by offering to top it up for him.

Eventually he roused himself and stood up from the table. He gargled a kind of a laugh and I noticed that he had only one tooth, a blackened monolith, in the front of his lower jaw. He slapped the oil-cloth covered table a resounding thwack with his ash-plant, like a man impatient to be about his business, tipped his cap to my mother and with a touch of old-world courtesy, gave her a little bow.

"I'm obliged to ye, ma'am," he declaimed, "and to your good self, Tom." With that he lost his balance and did a little Fred Astaire sideways in my direction and I heard myself saying, "Sure I might as well walk along with you for the air."

My father's face relaxed in gratitude. I held the door open. I wonder if the Good Samaritan felt as I did as we made our way across the fields that night. We imagine him moving to heavenly music, suffused with light from on high, as he did his work of mercy, but I dare say there were times when the man slipped from side to side on the donkey and the poor Samaritan had to nip round in time to push him back on, that he cursed the so and so and felt like throwing him back where he had found him on the Jericho road.

Badger negotiated fences with the skill of the consummate funambulist, not the one who darts efficiently from one side to the other in minimum time, but rather the one who staggers halfway across, as if by accident, and then wobbles about at the imminent hazard of breaking his neck, while the crowd below gasps in alarm. Miraculously he survives and the spectator realises that he has been in the presence of genius.

It is an established fact that drunks never hurt themselves in a fall, but there is every chance that they will hurt the person they fall upon. I kept a wary eye out at the fences. Badger stopped every now and again and attempted to light a cigarette. He lost a good few in the long wet grass before he fumbled one into his mouth and got a match to coincide with it. As soon as he got it going he removed it and used it to emphasise a point.

"Tell you somethin', Jamie."

He clutched at my shoulder. I smelt his breath. There was a kind of fish smell from his old coat. The glowing tip of the cigarette described a figure of eight in the darkness. "You're a good lad. Always said it."

I made no reply, regretting the impulse that had sent me out into the night.

"Always knew ye'd do well for yourself. The brains, ye see, the oul' brains." We stumbled a bit further on and clambered over a five-barred gate into a little rutted lane.

"You're grand," I said reassuringly, my hand hovering in anticipation behind his elbow. Grand is that amorphous no-man's land between very good and lousy. A husband tells his wife that she looks grand. There is no absolute need for a brown paper bag with two eye-holes. A young bride looks at her first home and pronounces it to be grand. She conceals her fear of penury and rising damp and the apprehension that she may have spancelled herself to a failure, in that nondescript word.

"Time was, be Jaysus, the Brehonys was very big around here."

I heard the ashplant whistle in the darkness as he indicated the extent of the ancestral estates.

"Oh yes, be Jaysus." There was no gainsaying him. The lane led us through the bottom fields below the hill. The swamp glistened away to our right. "Back in oul' god's time." Where had I heard that before?

The haunted house loomed darkly in front of us. It struck me that I had shown, not just exemplary charity, which I hope has been duly noted to my credit, but a kind of extraordinary courage, that I might not have shown if I had given the matter some forethought. Supposing he was mad. Supposing he fastened his sinewy hands around my throat as he had done to another. I felt a chill run down my spine. I could end up like the other poor devil, with the guards digging holes all over the property trying to locate my bones. And yet I had to go through with it. At a pinch I would probably have been a match for him if it came to a struggle.

I got him to the door. Even in the half dark I could see that the place had gone to the dogs. Weeds grew feet high through the tines of a hay-rake. The shed door hung from one hinge. The familiar smell of dung, the odour of prosperity, was significantly missing.

He paused and rattled at the latch. An old dog inside barked and thumped its tail against the door.

"I'll be off then," I said, glad to be rid of him.

"Tell me, Jamie," he said, putting his face close to mine, so that the whites of his eyes gleamed up at me. I realised that I was taller than he was. "Tell me somethin'. Why did she do it, at all?"

As far as I knew it was the first time he had ever mentioned her to anyone. In a way, I suppose, the answer was obvious. He had only to look in the mirror but, in the idiom of the day, I sidestepped the question.

"I haven't a clue," I said. "I really haven't a clue."

He said no more on the subject, but shuffled inside and I heard a match scraping. A light appeared inside and I concluded that he would survive for the time being. I decided to go on through the yard and come home by the road. I did not fancy going back past the old house by myself. The vane of the windcharger creaked overhead and gave me a start. The wind sighed through the struts. I set off briskly.

Badger had said it. I had done well for myself. Fergal was replete, like a big frog, content with his lot. Anto was happy in the bosom of his family, despite his precarious financial position, and I had the brains. But what I lacked was a clue, a sense of direction. I needed to find my lodestar.

There was a time when folk music was a minority interest of little commercial value. A few of the old stock survived, very often in straitened circumstances and transmitted their skills and their knowledge to a younger generation. I enjoyed a certain amount of it, without being an *afficionado*. The *sean nós* was a bit beyond me. I suspected that it might be heretical to say that authenticity does not always compensate for a lack of musical talent in some of its exponents. The *uileann* pipes however struck a responsive chord, not literally, I hasten to add, as I have no skill in that department. The very tone of the pipes suggested an age-old lament, a keen born of centuries of suffering. I am not, by the way, a morbid or melancholy type of person, but in the pipes I heard the *lacrima rerum* (quoting from Father Rice of course), the sadness that lies deep in all existence.

Suddenly there was an unprecedented upsurge of interest, a great burgeoning of folk music. A young generation rediscovered its wealth of traditional music and I fear, produced a lot that was meretricious and phoney. It would be invidious to claim authenticity for some and to condemn others, but in retrospect the real McCoy has stood the test of time. For a while every pub sprouted a ballad group, usually very hairy, who dragged their authenticity around like clubbed feet. Every song was learnt at the feet of a drunken tinker from Roscommon. Strapping lads and lasses feigned a tubercular lung and the last stages of alcoholism. The singer shook with the mandatory ague and sang of blood and battles and the fight for freedom.

But through this welter of dross, like a shimmering silver thread, the real thing survived. The spark as it were, was handed on to another generation and the others went their ways into deserved obscurity, revisionism or Nashville. The big money lay elsewhere, but money was never the main consideration of the true artist though not all artists, I understand, take as detached a view.

The archbishop warned us of the impending opening of the floodgates of immorality and what was to become the permissive society. Like many another, I trod water and waited. Maybe the man was right. There seemed at times a kind of desperate urge to prove that my generation had thrown off the shackles of a repressive conservatism. Perhaps every generation feels the same. An old gentleman wrote to *The Radio Times* (from which, incidentally, I had taken my chart of the cricket field, in more innocent times), complaining about the youth of today. I could just imagine him, moustache bristling with indignation, fought with Monty and all that rot, reaching for his fountain pen as undoubtedly, he had often reached for his swagger stick. 'What I can't understand about the younger generation', he wrote, 'is their confounded assumption that they discovered sex. In fact, I discovered it — in nineteen thirty-three.' Yes, by George, and I have to compliment him on his discovery. I followed in the footsteps of that intrepid pioneer and found it very much to my liking, provided there was no danger of complication.

The term 'one night stand' I always thought a bit of an exaggeration, 'a consummation devoutly to be wished', but now and again, I struck a little vein of ore and came close to forming what is called a meaningful relationship. I found the flat a great help in the pursuit of nubile young women but I also must admit to strategic withdrawals homewards when complications loomed.

I studied under a master, my employer, later to be my friend and partner, Harry, Howitzer to his acquaintances, Shaw. He had the money to indulge his concentric practices. I use that word to describe a distinguished eccentric, because by drawing circles on a map centred on Howie's residence, where he lived with his mother, I could have predicted the fortunes of his long succession of lady friends.

While his fervour burned with a clean pure flame, a fortnight in Spain or Paris was not out of the question. The writing was on the wall with a weekend in Courtown or Ballybunion and meeting for a drink in Drumcondra was the kiss of death to many a young hopeful. I saw them draw closer and closer to the epicentre and disappear into the vortex of his mother's disapproval and his own culpable indifference.

Corpulent and untidy as he was, I liked him for his candour and singlemindedness. Why he drove such a small car for a man of his size and obvious wealth, was always a mystery to me. It caused him, by his own say-so, many a difficult manoeuvre out on Dollymount beach on a dark night or up at the Pine Forest, when he brought the mott out to view the city lights. I think he imagined that a sports car contributed to a breezy devil-may-care image which made him irresistibly attractive to women.

He always maintained that the natural state of man is monogamous, despite all appearances, but that life is a pilgrimage in search of the ideal woman. His mother found him an ideal woman in the long run and saw to it that he ceased his quest. Based perhaps on his experience of the world, he monitors his children's comings and goings with a Victorian rigour and has been heard to say that youngsters nowadays have gone to the dogs.

I never could stand a row or recriminations, and yet I let myself in for them at regular intervals. My associations with young women always seemed to end in blame, much of it I would say, deserved. I was accused of selfishness and coldness, none of which I could deny, as my interest had become engaged elsewhere. I might at the time be grappling with some technical problem relating to my trade, which would absorb me for weeks and the last thing I wanted was emotion. In short order they went away and I was left to my devices and to my guilt.

Everyone had hoped that Vatican II would adapt to the consumer, drive in, throw-away society, particularly with regard to confession. A kind of spiritual sprinkler system could deal with large numbers at the same time. Guilt would self-destruct without any embarrassed mumbling in the dark. There was a bit of a turn-up in confession during the missile crisis, but generally people had another pint and waited fatalistically for the end. I trundled my guilt along to confession. I felt bad about hurting people. I served mammon, connived at covering the green fields with soulless housing estates. I neglected my aged parents and I drank too much. I was a worthless swine who should be flogged and forced to kneel in ashes. He asked me about sex which I thought very personal. What about all the greater evils? In the one area which I had enjoyed and where I had striven to give satisfaction, I was at fault. They always say 'ah!' when they think they have you. 'Ah! But my son you use people selfishly for your own pleasure.' He mentioned matrimony. I thought of my brother Anto, with the grey hairs appearing at his temples. Distinguished looking, people said. Like the rich young man in the gospel, I went away disconsolate.

As a nation we settled for commercial television. The great pageant of human life presented on the flickering screen has to be fragmented to fit in between the advertisements. The continuity announcers try to keep us in touch with what went before, smiling gamely through stories of war and natural disaster. The news-readers finish with the mandatory smirk as if trying to redress the damage they have done to our spirits. Even the weatherman assumes a ghastly rictus at the end of his dismal tale. American dramas end with a joke and an explanation for the feeble-minded among us, to leave us content and able to give our full attention to the commercial break. British dramas end just when you think the story is about to make some sense. Writing starts sliding up the screen and you sit wondering what it was all about. This is more intellectual. I found myself answering back to the television. No doubt this is a product of living alone. I corrected pronunciations and cavilled over points of argument, confounding the experts at every turn.

Television and music can be a disconcerting combination. I have seen fillings in the back molars of glamorous young female vocalists. I have no wish to do so. I would prefer if the cameraman would draw back a little and allow me to appreciate the full figure. The soaring voice of a tenor can lose some of its impact when you find yourself watching a tier of wobbly chins. Instant dislike can be taken towards the unctuous exponent of the stroll-down-memory-lane, as he leans his elbow on the piano and radiates wholesomeness at the audience. I had expected television to entertain me but so far it was nothing more than an irritant. It was making me old and crotchety before my time.

Then, through the miracle of modern television, I saw her again. It was a programme where traditional musicians blended the old sounds with a modern idiom. Old instruments like old dogs, learned new tricks. The presenter, a composer of considerable stature, introduced a rising new group who had made a big impact among the Irish communities in Britain and The States. There was further build-up and mention of recordings and suddenly I was looking at Kate and three of her brothers, The Sheehy Folk. I leaped forward and adjusted the volume. The picture flickered and became a grid of black bars. I thumped the set, as the makers recommend and she was back. There was no mistaking her, but she was no longer the girl that I remembered. She was now a tall young woman with, I thought, a touch of gauntness about her. Her hair was long and the studio lights shone through it, giving her that halo effect that I recalled so vividly. I remembered that she had been noted for her singing voice but never until that moment had I heard it. No doubt there was a deal of electronic trickery with echo-chambers and the like, but I felt the hair stirring on my scalp at the very timbre of her voice.

The song was in Irish, so I was not too sure of the meaning. Nevertheless the words were of secondary importance to the haunting melody. Chords chimed and mingled, dying away almost to nothing, and Kate carried a plaintive theme like a traveller in a ghostly landscape where strange shapes rose out of the mist and were subsumed back into it. The song was like a series of images, *sfumato*, a glimpse into the dreamtime. The final chords faded with the light and she became a silhouette, melting back into the reverberating darkness.

I pounded downstairs to the phone. The book, dog-eared and stained, lay on the floor. I flittered through it, looking for the number. The corners of the pages clung together as if in a conspiracy. Coins rattled in the box and I heard a voice. I explained that I wanted to speak to the young lady who had just finished singing. The impersonal voice faltered. I thought I heard a little laugh and then I was told that that particular programme had been pre-recorded during the previous summer. No. She could not give me any further information and thanked me, in a practised sing-song, for my enquiry.

I went upstairs again. "Meanwhile back at the bacon-factory," said a mechanical voice. Large anthropoid pigs with top hats and canes vied with each other in an effort to get through the factory gates, dying to be converted into rashers and sausages. "Pork will make you free," I snarled.

How was I to find her? It was typical of the way she used to appear, always taking me by surprise and then, fading away when it suited her. I thought I could possibly locate her through a record company if I could find her record, or perhaps through theatrical agents, although I knew little of showbusiness. From what I had seen of showbusiness people on television they all seemed to inhabit a zone of desperate optimism just on the brink of the big breakthrough. I doubted if anyone would have time to listen to a request that did not promise some immediate concrete reward. An agent, I imagined, would guard his client from outside interference with the tenacity of a priest's house-keeper. Nevertheless I had to try.

Thirteen

As my father neared retirement I spent a bit more time at home. They were a lonely old pair and liked to have someone to chivvy and fuss over, particularly in the mornings. In all parents there lurks the fear that their children, personifications of their love though they may be, will never grow up and stand on their own feet. Fathers particularly harbour this deep dread that their sons will lie in bed, growing and battening like enormous cuckoos to be a burden to their old age. There was of course no need for such a worry in my case, but the old atavistic fear persisted especially in the mornings. I was never great at getting out of bed and recall how I used to rattle my shoes on the lino to give him the impression of activity when he would shout up from below.

I blinked my eyes a couple of times and looked at the clock. It was five to eight. I heard his feet descending the stairs and knew that he had been shaking my shoulder.

"*Lift up Your* fucking *Hearts* and you're still lying there," he accused and I knew that something bad had happened. He never swore about such minor matters as missing a train or becoming unemployable. This was a serious occasion. The front door slammed and the knocker jumped a couple of times.

"What's all that about?" I asked, aggrieved.

My mother's face was white with shock. She twisted her apron in both hands.

"Badger was run over by the late goods last night," she said in a shaking voice. She snuffled and wiped her eyes with the hem of her apron. "Your father is very shook."

"Is he . . .?" I began, stunned. "Was he killed?"

She nodded. "Oh it's dreadful," she whispered. "The poor, poor man."

She sat down on a chair and began to sob silently. I patted her shoulder awkwardly and muttered some inanity.

There were people standing by the barrow-path and fresh sawdust was strewn on the sleepers. Who keeps those supplies of sawdust handy? I always wondered. In school they used to send out for some sawdust if a child got sick or lost his bowel control at the wrong time. I always imagined the sawdust man with his trusty blade, swinging into action at the word of an emergency. Two Guards were talking to my father and occasionally waving back the curious commuters whose dull routine had been enlivened by tragedy. People spoke in hushed tones and explained to each newcomer exactly what had happened.

My father looked pale and sad. He seemed to have dwindled over night.

"Terrible business," he said taking me by the elbow. I thought he was close to tears. "We found him about half-four this morning. They took him into Jervis Street but sure, he was stiff as a board, God help him."

"Stand back there," repeated one of the Guards as a reflex. The onlookers shuffled back two paces in deference to his authority and gradually encroached again. I glanced at the sawdust and the dark stains on the ground and turned away. I had no desire for further details. I sat down on a bench and put my head back against the cold brick wall. The clouds whirled overhead. A house-marten darted out of a shed and swooped low over the track. I watched his jinking flight.

My father sat down beside me and exhaled wearily. "He said to me one time, not so long ago, that he saw lights in the marsh and that they led him astray all over the place." He smiled sadly. "Poor old Badger. Maybe the gentry led him astray in the end." He produced a handkerchief and blew his nose vigorously.

"Do you think?" I said, humouring him. But they would never have gone near the iron rails.

"Ah, if only I'd seen him I could have done something to stop him," he went on.

"It would have happened one way or the other," I pointed out. "It was only a matter of time."

"Aye," he sighed. "The last of the Brehonys. It's all gone now." He raised his head and, following his gaze I saw the hill shining a vibrant green, topped by yellow gorse. The dark bulk of the old house stood out with startling clarity on the clear morning air. The wind-charger glinted in the light.

"All gone," I agreed. "I wonder how long they were there."

"Doesn't matter now, does it? It's that poor divil I feel sorry for. A terrible way to end."

"What will happen now?" I wondered aloud.

"I suppose we'll look after things. Your mother is the nearest thing he had to a relation."

"I don't mean that. I mean about the land."

"Oh, that will be fixed up very fast, I dare say. He was in up to his neck with the bank. It should fetch a good few bob."

For a brief moment I thought of buying the land. I could borrow the money. No one would lend me that kind of money. It was a momentary brilliant impossible dream and it died at birth. That, I thought, is the way of the world. Things change and we must accept the fact. I was not bound to the land by anything more than sentiment and a history of my own fabrication. Fantastically I imagined for that brief instant, that owning the hill might bring Kate back to me but then as if a cloud passed over the sun, I thought of Olford's hidden grave, I shivered.

The landscape painter paints his hedgerows a deep umber and Vandyke brown and then picks out the patches of light on the dark background, perhaps in acknowledgement of the dark malevolent forces that lie beneath the surface in the world around us. Green, the colour of innocence, merely masks the black reality. I felt the sadness envelope me and I looked at my father.

"It's no joke," I said, meaning it quite literally. He was uncharacteristically at a loss. The morning train roused him from his sombre contemplation. It rumbled and threw up clouds of steam.

"Changing to diesel on this line," he remarked gloomily, rising from his seat. There was no end to his tribulations.

With increasing prosperity I bought an apartment overlooking a small park and the grounds of a convent. I liked the builder's hoarding which stated succinctly 'If you lived here you'd be home now'. From my window I could look down on well kept lawns and exotic trees, planted centuries before, in an age of elegant leisure. Beyond was the convent and in one corner of their grounds, the nuns' cemetery, row upon row of small black crosses; no grandeur here in the face of death. I thought it a poor do that those who took vows of poverty in life and gave up everything should be denied a decent bit of stone for the passer-by to admire. It was carrying self-denial a bit too far.

I obtained the large twenty-five inch map of my home district and embarked on a project. I expanded the section of the map that dealt with Brehonys' Hill and the surrounding area and began to construct a model. If I could not own it in life I could at least reproduce it to scale and exorcise some of my old preoccupation. I debated whether to use the techniques of the architectural model, cutting thin sheets of cork to fit the contours, but in the end I opted for realism.

The project grew and began to occupy a sizeable part of my living room. It was in a sense, an utterly pointless exercise, incomprehensible to anyone but myself, but it exercised an increasing fascination and probably saved me a lot of money that I would have spent in propping up a bar in some hostelry. I selected pieces of sponge with the care a gourmet gives to his food and gradually planted my line of woodland in autumnal colours. I built walls and stiles with pebbles carefully selected and glued with epoxy resin. I pared matchsticks for fence posts and for the second time I whitewashed Badger's cottage, this time being careful to leave the little niche under the gable end.

In the end it was complete and fixed upright on the wall. By varying the lighting angles I could produce different times of day, the short shadows of noon and the long fingers of shadow stretching out at evening from the line of trees. My friends wondered why I went to such an amount of trouble but I maintained that it was a harmless pursuit and more importantly, that it kept me out of the pubs. This is always a clincher, especially with people who spend a lot of time in pubs.

My father retired and moved to a small house in the town. Some of his good spirits returned and he and my mother spent a lot of time with their grandchildren. Anto gave them a lot of his time and saw to it that they were rarely alone. He devised little jobs for my father, feigning incompetence himself. When I think of it, Anto always had time for others and took very little for himself. He made himself available as a coach for football and hurling and was rarely to be seen without an entourage of small and noisy children.

On my visits, which had become fewer and further between, I was always greeted as a person of some importance. My parents seemed to think it a big thing that I could spare them the time to come and visit, whereas I suspect, they took my brother somewhat for granted. I was driving my own car by this time and the journey, which I increasingly grudged, took anything up to forty-five minutes.

"I suppose you've noticed what's going on up at Brehonys' Bottoms," my father remarked one day.

"No," I replied. "What's that?"

"Oh, big changes. They're taking the hill away for gravel."

"What?" I replied. "Who's taking it away?"

"That fellow that bought the land. He has a contract with the corporation. They say he's making a fortune."

It was as if a cold hand had grasped my heart.

"They can't do that," I burst out. "Surely that's a protected site. Wouldn't the Board of Works have it registered?"

"You'd know more about that than I would," he said offhandedly. "You can see the big digger at work from the station. They started in there a few weeks ago."

I felt a kind of irrational panic, as if I personally was being robbed.

"I often go up to the signal box, just for a yarn," he went on wistfully. I had to see for myself. Right enough, from the platform I could see the top of an orange-coloured machine behind the hedgerows, and a small brown scar on the side of the hill. I drove around by the road past Sheehys' house and down the lane towards Badger's cottage. The road was strewn with muddy gravel which bore the tracks of many wheels. Across the land was a gate topped by barbed wire and a notice which declared 'No admittance, except on business'. The gate, that Saturday afternoon, was padlocked. I could see that there was a kind of nick taken out of the curve of the hill, but the old familiar features, the fort and the old house were untouched. I concluded that there was no real danger to the hill proper. Gravel pits were always opening and being abandoned after a few months. They could be interesting in their own right. It was intriguing to study the grain of the deposits and try to imagine how many generations of ice it had taken to lay the whole thing down. I could see very little from the car and, not having boots with me, a rare oversight, I decided to come back another time and have a stroll around.

On an impulse I called in on Dan Sheehy on the way back. The place had become even more wild than I ever remembered it, as if it were merging slowly back into the ground. The old Volkswagen lay like a great rusty cockroach in a clump of nettles. I introduced myself to Dan, who hardly seemed to have changed from when I had last seen him. For a moment he did not recognise me.

"Ah yis. The station-master's young lad," he said at length and scratched his head. "And what can I do for you?" He was sort of on his guard.

"Nothing," I assured him. "I was just passing and thought I'd look in."

"Aye," he nodded and waited.

"I was just wondering how the lads were getting on and Kate," I added casually, hoping that he would expand on the occasional laudatory mention in the newspapers.

"Aw, grand, grand," he said, not giving much away. "They're away in the States a lot of the time."

"I'd just like to write to them, if I had an address," I went on, "just to say hello."

"Aye," he seemed to think that very reasonable. "I wouldn't have an address though, or an'thin' like that. They're always on the move."

I could see that I was not going to get any change out of him. It was as if I was intruding on private ground. I retired, defeated.

"If you hear from them anyway, just say I said 'hello'," I said, backing away. "Nice to see you again, Mr Sheehy." I debated calling him Dan, but did not rule out a clip in the ear for familiarity.

"Aye," he said and scratched his head again. "I might do that."

On the way back to town an unaccountable gloom settled on me. It was time, I decided, to get out a bit more and have a few good scoops in convivial company. I drank gin that night which left me more depressed than ever.

Fourteen

"If you're ever buying a house in an estate like this," said my partner, portentously, "there are two things to be avoided, the site hut where the tea is made, and the place where they park the cement mixer."

He carried an air of authority with him and was always immaculately dressed, especially for formal occasions. "If you have to bawl somebody out, do it from behind a tie," he insisted. I could never keep up to his standards. "A reprimand has no force if it comes from an open-necked shirt." A dog is obeyed in a collar and tie, I mused, rephrasing Lear.

"The ground is so trampled around the tea hut that whatever poor so-and-so buys the site will never get a spade into the ground. If you get the cement mixer, your garden will be all gravel. You'll spend a fortune on peat moss." It was not an immediate problem for me and never likely to be one. I never purposely seek out unnecessary physical work like gardening.

The concrete mixer chuntered away in the background, an enormous machine built on the lines of an ancient seige mortar. The association of words intrigued me. Walls are raised up and razed down by mortars. A lorry interrupted my reverie. I stepped back and caught the driver's eye as he swung onto the site. I recognised him as a lad I had been to school with in the National School – always called the Nash (or perhaps Gnash, with good reason). He waved a greeting and I went over to say 'hello'.

He told me about the finding of a grave on Brehonys' Hill.

"That's right," he said, enjoying my reaction, "a grave. Tell you somethin', it put the heart across me."

So the story was out at last, I thought. Foul deeds will rise.

"Did they identify the body?" I queried. I had known it all along.

"Body, how are ye. There was loads of them. Well a good few anyway," he emended.

"What do you mean, a good few? Was it not just your man Olford?"

"Nah," he scoffed, "though funny like, I seen his oul' fella down there when the word got around. On a horse, he was. You know the way they always are, lookin' down his nose like, at people. I suppose he thought it was the quare fella."

"And it wasn't," I pressed.

"No, no, this was an ancient grave. Tell you what it was like. Did you ever see pictures of the concentration camps? All the bodies jumbled up like and a bulldozer shovellin' them into a pit. All stark naked and bones stickin' out."

"You mean you could make out skeletons?"

He paused and a strange look came into his eyes.

"Funny thing that," he said. "You wouldn't believe it."

He shuddered although the day was warm. "The chap in the digger was workin' just beside the old house. You know the old haunted house, as we used to call it."

"I know it well," I said. "Yeah, go on."

"He said he was going to knock it. Undermine it and let it collapse. Dangerous way of doin' it, but he likes to show off a bit. Sittin' up there with a cigar in his gob. Thinks he's fuckin' John Wayne, or someone like." This was some old grudge.

"Don't we all at times?" I interjected, trying to get him back on the track.

"Right enough," he admitted and gave a little laugh. "Anyway some of the ground just slipped out from under and there they were, all jumbled up like I said." He gestured expressively with the fingers of both hands, like the old game of the church and steeple, open the doors and there's the people.

"Your man stopped the digger and I declare to God, we heard a kind of a sigh. For a minute they seemed to be just lookin' at us an' then they faded away. No word of a lie. Men, women and children."

He spoke rapidly, keen now to impress me with the truth of his story. "I'm not kiddin'. There was only a pile of bones after a couple of minutes." I must have looked dubious.

"You can ask your man yourself, if you don't believe me. He said it must've been gas, maybe from the swamp, trapped in the hole, like. Maybe that preserved them. We heard it escapin'. That was what must've preserved them, till the air got at them like."

He could see that I was impressed. "Under the house, like?" I said, absorbed into his turn of phrase.

"That's right," he nodded. "Like a big rabbit burrow. Tell you what, more like a badger's set." He laughed a short mirthless series of grunts. "That's a good one, eh? A badger's set. I'd say there was dirty work there in the old days."

I was silent. So she had not been play-acting. Like a diviner, she had known they were there. She had felt their pain reaching down across the centuries, heard their cries and shared their fear. How was it that I had felt nothing? Yet I had had that strange, recurring dream, until funny enough, I had got rid of the key. I had almost forgotten that.

"What happened then?"

"Well the boss went for the Guards and the priest, like, though I suppose it was a bit late in the day. Wasn't it?"

I nodded. "You might say that."

"I'll bet that was why they always said the place was haunted."

"You could be right," I agreed, anxious now to get away. I wanted to sort out my thoughts.

"You should go and have a look for yourself," he said, climbing back into the cab. The engine revved and the back of the lorry began to rise. The gravel cascaded into a damp pile on the ground. The hydraulic lift gave a couple of convulsive jerks to dislodge the last few grains and the lorry slid out from under its load. The floor gleamed like a mirror, polished by friction.

"You'd want to get a move on," he shouted above the noise. "We're takin' fifty loads a day out of it." He waved and rumbled away over the rutted ground. The hydraulic lift subsided gradually and the lorry reverted to its more familiar outline.

I rang a friend in the Board of Works.

"Do you know anything about Brehonys' Hill?" I asked directly, even giving him the map reference.

"Not much," he admitted. "I think there's some kind of a field monument marked on it, but I don't think it's a protected site."

"Can you slap a preservation order on it? Did you know there was a major archaeological find there only the other day?"

Nobody argues with that kind of terminology.

"No I didn't," he admitted. "Was the Museum informed?"

"Couldn't say. I've only just heard about it."

"Hmm," he mumbled. "If we tried to put an order on every site in the country, we'd spend our lives in the High Court. You don't slap these orders on just like that."

"It'll be too late, if you don't hurry."

"I tell you what. I'll get onto the Museum and see what they know about it."

I had to leave it at that and went back to work. The following day I drove down myself, fully expecting to find the place roped off and the hill swarming with archaeologists, like Schliemann's Troy. There was a Morris Minor parked beside the cottage. I pulled on a pair of boots and headed down towards the gravel pit.

The old house was gone, shivered into its component parts and bulldozed aside into a pile of stone and shattered timber. Where it had stood there was a cliff, cut sheer into the hillside, with fans of fallen gravel at the base. The roots of grass were visible in the scant few inches of soil along the rim. The pine trees still clung to the brink. There was a flowing line of marley clay running across the face of the cliff, a fine clay almost like plasticine, fine enough, I concluded, to trap gas or water as the case might be. Already there was a pool gathering in the deepest part of the pit.

There were two men talking to the driver of the digger. One was pointing at the cliff and shaking his head and the other was nodding in a kind of counter point. The driver stood, chewing on a cigar and contributing very little to the discussion. As I approached, one of the men shrugged and made a very expressive gesture of resignation, holding his hands out, palms upwards, like a French film actor. He turned away and thrust his hands into his pockets. As he passed me he muttered the one word 'troglodytes' with astonishing venom. He wore a green combat jacket with many pockets.

So that was it, I thought, not catching his meaning at first. He had obviously made a rapid diagnosis of the situation, I concluded that he was from the Museum. He clumped away up the lane obviously in a foul humour. The other two regarded me warily. Another trouble maker.

"Morning," said the man in the suit, obviously the boss. "What can I do for you?"

"Morning," I replied. "I was just wanting to have a look around."

"Any particular reason?" he asked with a touch of aggression.

"I'm from the Income Tax," I said lightly. "Just wanted a look around, you know."

A spasm of pain distorted his features and the blood drained from his cheeks. The driver looked on with interest and chewed on his cigar. He wore a peaked baseball cap, which definitely enhanced the image.

"Income Tax," croaked the boss and reached into his pocket for his cigarettes. Stall at all costs.

"Nah," I laughed, "I'm only kiddin'. I used to live around here and I heard about the grave."

Relief flooded the boss's face. He all but fell on my neck. He laughed heartily and his colour returned.

"Income Tax," he guffawed, "that's a good one."

We were brothers in arms against the depredations of an unjust and tyrannical government. We knew what it was to have the bread taken out of our mouths, the shirts off our backs. He slapped me on the shoulder. "Ye had me there, all the same," he acknowledged generously.

The driver joined in the general bonhomie.

"Sure they came from all over," he said, "took bits of bones for souvenirs. I'll say one thing. They had great teeth in them days. They all had great mouthfuls of teeth." This detail impressed him enormously.

"Your man there," said the boss jerking his thumb in the direction of the lane, "wanted us to stop work. Sure Jays, we'd be bankrupt, waitin' for that shower to finish their programme. Sure they'd be at it for years."

He looked at me for corroboration. I nodded. No cock crew.

"What happened anyway to the grave?" I asked in the forlorn hope of seeing something definite.

The driver pushed his cap back on the crown of his head, pulled insouciantly on the almost shredded cigar and exhaled.

"Ran the fuckin' digger through it," he snorted "and the oul' house fell down on the lot. Only thing to do really."

"How far do you intend to go?" I enquired.

"Ah," said the boss," the whole thing is comin' out. The quicker t better or we'll have your man," a jerk of the thumb towards the lane, "on our house. Why don't you have a look around? We'll be havin' a cup of tea in a few minutes." I declined the offer. I had no wish to see the fort. The heart was torn out of the place. I took my leave.

"Income Tax," I heard him chuckle. "That's a good one, all right." The digger began again, revving and subsiding as if unsure of what it was about. It seemed to carry on an argument with itself, moving forward and back, the bucket blade gouging into the cliff. Cascades of gravel slithered downwards. I stepped aside in the lane to avoid a lorry. Mud like thin cement splashed on my boots and a few spatters reached my well creased trousers. I got into my car, reversed out and went to see my parents. They looked on my visit as an unexpected treat. My mother said that I looked tired and should take a bit of a holiday.

Fifteen

I went down to Newgrange once to see the sun shining into the chamber at the winter solstice. My friend in the Board of Works wangled it for me, just as people probably did at the time that the place was built. I went on the day after the solstice, not qualifying as a dignitary, but the effect was much the same. I drove down over icy roads, before even the grit lorries had been out. I took great care and got a pain in the back of my neck from the tension.

The country was bound in a white frost. It was indeed the dead of winter. I counted the small creatures squashed by the previous day's and night's traffic. It seemed that they could never adapt to our coming and going, or even have the sense to stay in their hedgerows. It was a wonder to me that any wild creatures could survive, given this daily and nightly carnage.

The tide was low at the Boyne. The roots of a fallen tree stuck up out of the water like a gnarled and withered hand. There was a sheet of ice on the canal. It was hereabouts that Aengus the old magician had come to land his fish and gain knowledge, only to be cheated of his triumph at the last minute. Here also the fugitive lovers Dermot and Grainne, came to seek his advice, a complex set of instructions that left their names dotted like lichen spots on every standing stone throughout the land. There was a story of love and implacable hatred to rival anything the Greeks had to offer. To be honest, I was a bit cynical about the whole business. It seemed to me that any competent architect could devise a window for the sun to shine through on any particular day. All it took was a wooden framework that could be offered up and shifted around until they got her dead on. A good jobbing carpenter with a few helpers could knock the whole thing together in jig time. The tourist people like to make a ballyhoo about anything old. Just lob the stones around the framework. Simple. We were checked off the guide's list and conducted over the crunching white grass to the entrance of the tomb.

"We had a marvellous display yesterday," he assured us. "There were people from all over the world. Photographers too and people from the television." Newgrange, I reflected sourly, officially existed at last, now that it had been on television.

"Still," he assured us, "we should do pretty well today."

We trooped inside, crouching unnecessarily low for much of the way down the passage. There was no doubt that it was solidly built. I cast a professional eye on the lintels and the corbelled roof. Not a sign of damp anywhere. They certainly knew their job.

The light was switched off and we waited in darkness. There was a tendency to make jokes. I looked at my watch. The sunrise was late by my reckoning. There was a bit of a glow in the passageway, but nothing to write home about. As if reading my thoughts the guide pointed out that the sun had to rise above the hill on the far side of the river.

A hush descended and people talked in whispers. The light in the tunnel strengthened and became a glowing amber. It was as if a blade reached into the darkness of the tomb. The light crept inch by inch across the sanded floor and we watched it in silence, our faces lit eerily from below. It penetrated the inner chamber and played for a long moment on the strange rock-carvings, chevrons and spirals, then, as if completing its task, it withdrew slowly, and left the chamber. The passageway dimmed as the world spun and the year turned the corner. There was little talk as we filed out into the ordinary sunlight.

"Oh we had all sorts here yesterday," the guide was saying again, proud of his wares. "An ambassador or two. A couple of professors. And the day before we had the Sheehys, that folk group, taking photographs for their new record, or so they said."

It was just my usual luck. Always in time to be late, as they say. I left the car by the river and walked along a path through the woods, waiting for the ice to thaw. It was very peaceful and I felt strangely at ease and confident as I drove back to town.

I bought the record as soon as it came out. *The Wanderer*, it was called, subtitled *Songs of the Dispossessed*.

There were songs of bravado and chicanery where tinkers put one across on the settled folk. There was a Romany plaint, with a backing like a violin bow being drawn across a raw nerve. There were songs of loss and of moving on, the story of refugees everywhere. Her voice carried the story, sprightly at times, but more often with a rending anguish that aroused not anger, but a terrible sense of waste. You would hardly say that you enjoyed the record but you remembered it as an experience.

Her photograph adorned the sleeve; soft and diffused, with the light, as I always pictured it, behind her. The photographer used all his subtle trickery to suggest a mystery, but he need not have gone to such lengths. She had mystery enough in her own right. I stood the picture on a book-case and contemplated it.

That summer the trouble that had been threatening in the North boiled over yet again. Like a volcano that lies dormant for a generation or so, the pressure built up and erupted, scattering the forces that tried to hold it down. The airwaves were filled with shrieks and shouting and the television showed in stark black and white, the ugliness of bigotry and violence. Stones littered the streets and blood ran down foreheads. Black figures fought and hurled missiles in front of blazing houses. We were told that we would not stand idly by.

A man trapped by the security screen on his shopfront, burned to death, while his neighbours cheered. The picture of a human being clawing at the red-hot metal nemesis that he had put there to give him peace of mind, has stayed with me ever since. I cannot recall his name. I could not say which side he belonged to or whether, by somebody's grotesque arithmetic, he deserved to die. He died and the onlookers laughed. Humour is about it happening to somebody else.

"We got nine of the bastards anyway," remarked my friendly neighbourhood newsagent.

"What was that?" I asked rooting for some change. He tapped the folded newspaper.

"Pogroms," he said. "I remember well in the twenties. At it again they are." The picture showed the, now all too familiar, scene of a street in flames.

"Twelve Catholics killed last night, but we got nine of the bastards this time." We, it seemed, were still three down and starting with a backlog going back several centuries.

"Only thing for it," he went on, "blow them all to hell out of it, back where they came from."

He interrupted his analysis to deal with a small child who had a shilling to spend. These deliberations took quite a while. "Two penny mice and a snake." The customer put his finger in his mouth and hopped from one foot to another in an agony of indecision. "And two of them."

In fact it was not a shilling any longer. It had been downgraded to five new p., a piece of *léger-de-main* with which I have never been able to come to terms. I reached over the child's head, put my money on top of a sweet jar and made my escape. The Final Solution, it seemed, was making a come-back.

I argued the toss with my partner to see what he made of it all.

"We're on very thin ice at the best of times," he said thoughtfully.

"But I mean, how can ordinary people do these things to each other?"

"I suppose, if you think you're in the right or if you're scared enough you'll do anything."

"Or if you have the power," I suggested.

"There's enough hate up there to keep them at it for a while."

"Right then, let me ask you something. Do you see yourself taking sides? I mean, if it came to a war, would you join up?"

He swivelled his stool around from his drawing board and looked down at where his belly hung out over his belt.

"I'll put it this way," he laughed, "if they need me for their army it can only mean that they're already bollixed."

I had to laugh at his attitude, but I felt deep down that things could only get worse.

I had to change my barber. It had less to do with tonsorial elegance than with the sad aftermath of a topping-out ceremony. The client was an insurance company and the ceremony took place on top of a new office block, a minor addition to the Dublin skyline. Property was booming, particularly office property and figures were bandied gleefully about concerning the rents per square foot and the annual cost of a waste-paper basket. The utilitarian box was the shape of things to come. This one was made of prefabricated sections faced with decorative cladding, which later turned deciduous and involved a lot of complex litigation – a painful experience.

Presumably the actuaries, those rare birds who perch near the top of the tree in every insurance company, have calculated the risks entailed in topping-out ceremonies, receptions to launch annual reports and similar functions which discharge inebriated and smiling free-loaders onto the streets just in time for the rush-hour traffic. I stepped gingerly onto the street, my feet, it seemed, just barely reaching the ground. Another satisfied client. It was too late to think of going back to the office. The street canted slightly to one side and I made the necessary adjustments to my trim. No ballast aboard, that was the problem. Ritz biscuits and anchovies do not constitute a proper meal. There is a limit to the number of olives you can ingest in an afternoon.

A telephone kiosk slid gracefully by. People hurtled towards me, as if out of the eye of a hurricane and a newsboy stepped out to offer me a paper. It was like the Hollywood convention when the new show goes on tour, a speeding train with, inexplicably, a newspaper whirling in front of it. 'Smash hit in Schenectady. Sensation in Buffalo', with tension setting in in St. Louis and estrangement by the time it reaches Chicago. Everything works out happily after a Broadway run.

It was raining and, without an umbrella, I could hardly dance through the puddles, *à la* Kelly. Suddenly I recognised my barber's shop, a haven of comfort, a retreat, where I could pause for reflection. I had been cultivating him for years. With him there was no need for conversation. Minor meteorological details were not thrashed out at great length. Tactics and the contagious lunacy of the Irish selectors could be passed over in silence. The great events of the day were nodded through.

I dozed off in the chair and came to, chuckling at something or other.

"Give it a wash?" he suggested, breaking his Carthusian silence.

"O.K." I agreed, without thinking.

My head was pushed forward over the basin and he attacked my scalp like a demented phrenologist. The head went up and down rapidly. Water swirled before my eyes. Great dollops of lather plopped into the basin. The anchovies within groaned for their native element and made a burst for freedom. A sizeable part of my life passed before my eyes, all the plunder of the afternoon, a terrazzo of canapés, olives, an interesting selection of cheeses, purple grapes on a field of dazzling lather. I gripped the sides of the basin and gawked in abject misery and humiliation.

My father's words came into my mind. 'Never mix the grain and the grape'. It was too late. 'And did the earth move?' they ask on significant occasions. Verily, it moved for me. I gripped the basin like Captain Ahab. The storm raged about me. 'Thar she blows'.

The barber darted his hand across and pulled the plug. A maelstrom spiralled in the basin and I bent in one last, racking paroxysm. Tears blinded my eyes as I stood carefully upright. He handed me a towel and flicked my shoulders with a little brush.

"Will that be all, sir?" he enquired, Jeeves-like, but I was sure there was a flicker of sadness in his mandarin eyes, a twinge more of disappointment than reproach. Wordlessly I shook my head, thrust some money into his hand and fled into the life-restoring rain.

Understandably, I had to change my barber. The new man ran a modest establishment, with dog-eared linoleum and a few bent-wood chairs perpetually on the verge of collapse. Bent-wood chairs last forever, possibly because nobody trusts them. Tilt a bent-wood chair backwards and it serves notice to quit.

There were magazines of venerable age, with the page corners individually curled, as if by craftsmen; *Time*, who write to me regularly offering to make me a more interesting and erudite person for half the normal price, *Newsweek*, *Time*'s brasher cousin, and a battered copy of *Life*, still obsessed with the comings and goings of leopards and baboons.

I mused in the afternoon sunlight, while a desultory conversation went on between the barber and the occupant of the chair. I transposed the *Life* photographs to the *Time* political articles and vice versa. It made very little difference. I mined further into the pile and came up with *National Geographic*. It had suffered a severe spinal injury and had lost its cover. I looked at the advertisements and resolved that someday, I too would possess a zoom lens. The years fell away as I flicked through the pages. Mount Palomar observatory was the nearest thing to a breast in the whole magazine. Obviously they had fallen on evil days. Where were the intrepid reporters of yesteryear? Did expense accounts no longer stretch as far as Bora Bora? It is scant consolation to schoolboys that the Tennessee Valley Authority has created a thousand miles of navigable waterway, forcing Hill-Billies to abandon their mules and moonshine in favour of sleek Chris Craft and Jack Daniels on the afterdeck. Who cares if the Swedes, after a winter of angst and Bergman films, escape to the idyllic peace of Gotland, to repair their drooping spirits?

'Time for Gotland', said the article and I read on, glad that there were two others ahead of me in the queue. The old harbour at Visby had seen it all. From this small island, according to tradition, the Goths had originated and had gone forth to shake the Roman Empire to its foundations. Hither came the Runic pirates, returning from Byzantium with gold and spices and the riches of the Orient, sailing the great rivers and making long and dangerous portages over the watershed of Europe.

The shaven men came here with their new religion. The princes of the House of Hans came here to divide the herring fisheries and to plan war on kings and emperors. But Gotland is no longer the hub of the world. The storms pass it by. Its citizens cultivate geraniums in terra-cotta pots and keep their houses bright and clean. Visitors stroll through the old streets or hike across the high peatlands.

I looked again at the photographs. The peatlands were just like Wicklow, long stretches of scarred peat workings, a deep sepia base with streaks of green and ochre. Low purple hills lined the background. Picture postcard cumulus clouds sailed in the blue. An empty road stretched ahead of two rucksack-burdened figures. Time for Gotland indeed. I realised that I wanted to get away, to be entirely alone, to drift down through Wicklow at my own pace, stopping and starting as the whim took me, in the hope that the sheer purposelessness of it all would allow some pattern to emerge in my life.

Sixteen

I followed the Military Road with an echo of Judy Garland ringing in my head. I stopped at the Lemass cross on the shoulder of the Featherbed Mountain and, from that point, a kind of melancholy descended on me. That cross is now destroyed, not by mindless vandals, I suspect, but by someone motivated by a deeper, more sinister, malice, a retroactive revenge. Not satisfied with the original murder he must return and obliterate the memorial.

The Military Road led me on over high moorland where lonely men probed at the bog with spades, and down beside a dizzying waterfall into the leafy stillness of Glendalough. The sombre quiet of the place suited my mood. It was here that the hermit, Kevin, came to spend a life of prayer and maceration by the silent lake. A greater penance awaited him though, as misfits, imitators and assorted devotees flocked to follow his example. No doubt he ended his days chairing committee meetings and replying to points of order. My meditations were disturbed by the smell of chips, which reminded me that I was hungry, and by the arrival of a bus-load of tourists, mostly Japanese, with elaborate looking cameras.

I moved on. I had the road to myself. Signs warned of a military firing range. I hoped that that was not the reason for the absence of other human beings in the area. I found that I was hunching in my seat and was aware of a pain in the back of my neck. No field guns thundered as I passed. I was not a worthy target, it seemed. 'Who goes there? Friend or foe?' It really is a very stupid question. I passed Aughavannagh, a hamlet no longer than its name, and came down into the spectacular cleft of Glenmalure, the lair of the gallant Michael

Dwyer and his mountain men. It was easy to see why Wicklow had always been a breeding ground of rebellion and why a military road had become necessary. Michael, I read subsequently, packed it in when his hiding place was penetrated and became a sergeant in the Queensland police; poacher turned gamekeeper if ever there was one. I wondered what happened to his mountain men. I realised that I had hardly spoken a word all day and imagined that my power of speech would atrophy from disuse. I went into a pub in Bunclody and ordered a drink. Two disconsolate old men were alternately looking into half empty stout glasses and watching a small black and white television which was set at an angle above the bar. An electronic Angelus bell rang from the screen and an angel knelt to the Virgin.

The music introducing the news is always ominous and immediately it was clear that something appalling had happened. A massive car bomb had devastated a Northern village. Estimates varied from six hundred to a thousand pounds of high explosive. Rubble and glass littered the street and naked rafters showed against the sky. Lights flashed and sirens wailed. The newsreader warned us that some of the scenes would be disturbing. A policeman shovelled pieces of a dismembered body into a plastic sack. I noticed that he used a navvy. It was a shining, brand new one and he handled it awkwardly, holding the mouth of the sack open with one hand. He had trouble with an unidentifiable lump and made several attempts to scoop it up, eventually succeeding by trapping it against the kerb. There were dark streaks on the bright new blade. The camera shifted to the twisted husks of burnt out cars and eventually to the eye-witnesses and the freak survivors. We were reassured by the observation that it could have been very much worse. In fact a great many people had been lucky.

One of the six people killed was a grandmother. Two were children. In the insane logic of terrorism that was not too good. Fortunately the other three were men, one of them a policeman. All in all, it could have been a deal worse. I wondered which of them had been scraped up with the navvy.

"Mother of Jaysus," said one of the men at the other end of the bar. I lost whatever need I had felt for conversation and drove on into the gathering dusk. In the darkness I drove carefully over the gap of Idrone where Strongbow had hacked his way into Leinster. I stopped for a while at the top of the pass and got out for a breath of air. I listened for the ghostly thunder of iron-shod hooves and the clink of armour. Perhaps the spirit of my old friend Thomas de Barneville was about, reliving his former triumph, but there was no sound but the low soughing of the wind funnelling between the mountains.

I woke next morning in a little room that overhung a stream. The room jutted out of the second storey of the house, like an afterthought. The stream purled below the window and combed over a little weir. Bright succulent weeds clung to the crevices in the stonework. For a moment I could hardly recollect where I was. There was a clattering of utensils downstairs and I realised that I had not eaten for almost a whole day. A solid breakfast of porridge and a fry, cholesterol to offset the beneficial effects of the oatmeal, and I was ready for the road again.

It struck me that I was only a couple of hours' drive from my old school and having nothing definite in mind I decided to have a look at the place. It is a truism that one should never go back, but even so, I was amazed by the changes. The monks had withdrawn from the educational process and had devoted much of their land to forestry. They also ran an experimental mountain farm, specialising in sheep as the first Cistercians had done a thousand years before. The demand for vellum though, has dropped off since those days.

There were no familiar faces in evidence and I was told that the priests that I remembered had long since been gathered to their reward. I declined the offer of lunch, remembering cabbage, and retraced my path down the mountain through glades of Transylvanian conifers, until I came to the village.

The newsagent's shop was still there, still with the old name over the door, in raised ceramic letters. She had never got around to changing it to O'Meara, it appeared. Perhaps like changing a boat's name, all the luck would have changed with it and the goodwill, a negotiable commodity, would have leaked out under the door. On impulse I went inside. A little bell rang behind me and an old woman shuffled out from an inner room.

"I hope I'm not disturbing you," I began politely, feeling about fourteen years of age, "but I was passing and I just thought I would ask after Mr O'Meara. He used to teach me abroad," I added, lapsing into the local argot and jerking my head in the direction of the mountain.

She put her head to one side like a bright-eyed old jackdaw.

"Master O'Meara, the teacher?" she queried and I wondered how many O'Mearas she had in stock.

"That's right," I nodded, narrowing it down a bit.

"Ah, yes." The matter had been clarified to her satisfaction.

"I just wondered how he might be keeping," I added, approaching the matter obliquely. It is very bad form not to know who is dead and who is not. Our local politician, a noted hand-shaker and funeral attender enquired twice after the health of one of his constituents. 'And how is your father?' he said, extending his hand. 'He's dead,' replied the son. Somewhere or other a malfunction in the old campaigner's memory bank prompted him to ask the same question a fortnight later, to be told, 'He's still fuckin' well dead'. Definitely no vote there, not even a floater.

She eyed me again, deliberating and said: "You can ask him yourself. He's out the back."

She led me through a store room and a dark old kitchen, shuffling ahead of me and pushing cats aside with her slippers. In among amazonian bean rows I saw my old teacher, or at least a smaller, more wizened version of the eccentric old codger. He still affected the linen jacket and an elegant Panama. Like Henry Morton Stanley I strode forward through the towering vegetation and extended my hand. Brilliantly coloured macaws screeched in the treetops. Spider monkeys flitted from branch to branch. Far off on the Savanna, I heard the coughing roar of the king of beasts, Mr O'Meara I presume.

"I don't know if you remember me sir; James Nugent, Jamie."

He blinked against the light and looked closely at me.

"Ah, yes, Nugent. Of course, of course. Got a terrible bang on the head if I recall. I remember your brother too. Older than you, wasn't he?"

"No, that was . . ." I began, eager to clear up the confusion, but he went on rapidly.

"The old place has changed of course. Wouldn't recognise it now."

He wrung my hand again. "Yes, I remember you two very well. Given up the hurling by now, I suppose."

"Oh yes, this long time," I agreed, seeing my identity slipping into obscurity. The moment of correction had passed and I was now put in the absurd position of not wanting to enlighten him for fear of being exposed as an impostor, masquerading as my obviously more admirable older brother. I must admit to a sharp sense of disappointment.

"Yes indeed. Mighty men, both of you, as I recall."

I considered declaring myself again, but feared that even then, he still might not remember me. He continued to fiddle about with the beans, draping some of the drooping pods over the strings. I stood respectfully, waiting for him to finish. He had a good crop there, I noted. Eventually he drew me to a rickety wooden bench beside the back wall and sat down, fanning himself with the Panama.

"Very hard to keep things in order," he remarked, "especially this time of year."

"That's what you always used to say," I said smiling. "You see I haven't forgotten everything you taught us."

The corners of his eyes crinkled and I saw that he was pleased.

"That bang on the head must have loosened up some grey matter after all," he chuckled. "I remember now. You're the fellow who wrote me the piece about the cinder heaps. Cheeky little so and so, you were."

I was not sure which of my *personae* answered to this description and decided to leave the credit with Anto.

"They flourish on Mount Etna, you know," he said absently.

Flourish is a favourite word of scholars. The Celts flourished in Ireland for a thousand years. The Egyptians flourished for much longer, but nobody ever tells us exactly what they were flourishing or why.

"What do?" I asked.

"Those weeds you wrote about. The yellow ones you see along the railway tracks. They take a great hold on ground like that."

"The forest," I prompted. "What do you make of all this business in the North?"

He sighed and crossed his legs. I noticed that he wore galoshes, almost a collector's item nowadays.

"Very sad," he said to my disappointment. I had expected some illuminating comment at best, or at least, an off-beat observation on which to hang a line of discussion.

"Very sad," he said again. "Look at that garden there. Pleasant, isn't it?" I nodded.

"You must put a lot of work into it."

"At a rough guess there are fifteen million insects in my quarter of an acre, all tearing each other apart, crunching each other's limbs." He clenched his fist. "Squeezing the life juices out of each other." There was a sudden ferocity in his voice. "What about that then?"

"I don't know," I mumbled. "I don't quite follow."

"We're at the same business," he said urgently, "only more so. We have the intelligence to organise the process."

"I see," I nodded, not so sure that I did see.

"The human race is the most destructive of all species. We are, if you like, a plague infesting the planet. It will take millions of years for the earth to recover from us."

"But what about progress?" I interjected lamely. "Father Rice used to say..."

"With all due respect to Father Rice, *de mortuis* and all that, he spoke a great deal of tripe. As far as he was concerned, if it happened long ago, that made everything respectable. Give me one of his heroes that wasn't a raving egomaniac."

I was silent.

"Mind you I wouldn't have said this to you when we were colleagues. Thieves falling out and so on, but I could never take all his ecclesiastical certainties. Always handing down his pronouncements."

"I never saw him in that light," I replied, feeling disloyal to the meticulous old priest. "I always thought he had a fairly open mind."

"Hmmh," he grunted leaving his thoughts unsaid. "This Northern business though, is just a sideshow. Some day we'll blow the whole shooting match to smithereens, more than likely."

"You don't hold out much hope, I'm afraid," I said feeling the melancholy enveloping me again. "Are there any sane people left in the world?"

"Maybe just the two of us, James, that we can sit down here and talk like intelligent men. There is a small voice of sanity in the North, but God help them, they will attract more hatred than the gunmen. Give it fifty years and we'll be singing ballads about what went on yesterday."

"I dunno," I demurred.

He shuffled again and looked at his feet.

"Maybe I'll show you something," he said, almost shyly, like a schoolboy offering to show a drawing or a rare bird's egg.

"Sure, sure," I said feigning interest. "What is it?"

"Just an idea of mine that I've been toying with." He stood up stiffly and led the way along a scuffed gravel path to what I had taken to be a series of cloches. Under the glass was a trough of green scummy water, above which hung several panels which looked suspiciously like the insides of an old fridge. An electric motor hummed inside a tea crate. Condensation ran down the panels and was caught in a length of guttering which allowed it to trickle through a hole in the glass and drip into a saucepan on the ground outside.

"The prototype," he said, looking sideways at me. "My water purifier."

"Ah," I said, "a water purifier. I see."

"That's right," he went on, gaining confidence. "On a big enough scale it could desalinate sea water and make the deserts productive."

I bit the corners of my mouth to prevent a smile. There was no doubt about it.

"I see," I repeated, at a bit of a loss. I glanced at my watch. "Is that the time? I should have been on my way ages ago."

I think he was disappointed by my reaction. Perhaps he had hoped that I might, as the only other sane person in the world, have collaborated with him on the greening of the Sahara. A bang on the head made Augustus John into a genius and opened the secrets of the universe to Isaac Newton. St. Paul had changed his ways after similar treatment, but Mr O'Meara had got the wrong man. I turned the car homeward and found myself smiling. 'They're all mad but me and thee, lad,' as the Yorkshireman says. 'And even thee's a bit touched.'

As I drove in a leisurely manner down the switchback road that allows a glimpse of the sombre, secretive upper lake, it appeared to me that Upper and Lower Loughs Bray were like neighbours that at some time or other had had an irrevocable tiff and had severed all communication, or perhaps, as they bore the same name, they were brothers or more likely sisters, lakes being undoubtedly feminine, who had had words. Words are such small matters, but inserted in the tiniest crevice, they work their ways in and expand slowly, but inexorably, destroying the fabric of relationships.

The lower lake was still and dark, with the reflection of Kippure standing vertical in the great black depth. It would be easy to believe that the lake was bottomless. The blackness belied the cheerful sound of the water as it escaped through boulders to rush down into the valley. It was a sombre place. I thought I might stretch the legs.

A tinker woman in a plaid shawl sat on a boulder by the lakeside. A young girl, presumably her daughter, played among the rocks, jumping across narrow straits of water to the outermost rocks where she knelt and peered into the depths. Not for the first time, I wished for a zoom lens. The plaid figure was reflected, a semitone darker, in the lake. The child jumped like a gazelle. She stopped to brush back a strand of hair that fell persistently in front of her eyes, with a movement that was oddly familiar.

I began to veer away from them to avoid being accosted with the threat of prayers in return for largesse. Giving and refusing can be equally embarrassing. Perhaps if they said the prayers first and handed you a chit. The Tibetans have the whole business down to a fine mechanical process. A prayer wheel would look well at the top of Glencree.

"That's a brutal hair-cut," said the tinker woman and I felt goose bumps. She laughed, the old throaty laugh and pushed the shawl back from her head. The hair was darker than I remembered it, with here and there, a lighter strand of incipient greyness. Lightnings of apprehension speared inside me. In a second she would vanish. The place had a bad reputation. She would change into a crone and drag me down into the weedy depths.

"You look as if you've seen a ghost," she laughed.

"A ghost? No, no. Not at all."

I realised that I had been staring open-mouthed.

"It is you, isn't it?" I asked, aware of the inanity.

"Certainly is," she said, rising and coming towards me.

In the films it would have been slow motion, giving me time to think; music; a diffused image against the sunlight; flowing semi-opaque chiffon and a soaring crescendo of strings as we embraced.

I shook her hand. May Allah strike the member from me. I grasped her outstretched hand and wrung it as she reached out, I think, to embrace me. I clung to her hand until I became self-conscious and then dropped it awkwardly.

"Hello again," I said feeling like a twelve-year-old.

"Jamie," she said, speaking my name for the first time. "Little Jamie. You're not still spying on me, are you?"

I blushed. "I never spied on you."

"I'm only kidding." She took my hand again and held me at arm's length. "You've changed a bit, haven't you?"

"That's an understatement. But you haven't," I lied.

Her smile flickered for an instant.

"How long has it been? Ten, twelve years?"

"A bit more," I could have told her to the day and the hour but there was no reason why she should know how important it was to me.

The child had come over out of curiosity. She looked up at us and pushed the hair back from her face. I felt a stab of jealousy. Kate drew the girl close and looked at me steadily.

"Ruth, this is an old friend of mine, Mr Jamie Nugent. Say hello to Mr Nugent."

"Not so much of the old," I said, taking the child's warm wet hand in mine. "Hello, Ruth. I'm very pleased to make your acquaintance.

Ruth was an Olford, even to the cow's lick of hair that troubled her, but there was also the old Sheehy wildness there, a march hare look about her, as if poised for sudden flight.

"Hello Mr Nugent," she said and looked at her mother. "Is Mr Nugent the boy you told me about before?"

"Jamie," I said. "Mr makes me sound very old."

"That's right. We knew each other when we were children. Now," she said, turning back to me and taking me again by the hand, "you must tell me all about yourself. Sit down here and fill me in on the details."

She spread the shawl on the rough grass and sat down, patting the space beside her by way of invitation. The child went back to her exploration of the lichen-spattered boulders.

I sat down and rested my elbows on my knees. I put a blade of grass in my mouth and chewed the end of it.

"I'm afraid I'm a very dull dog," I began, half apologetically. "Nothing much to report."

"You're an architect, aren't you?"

"How did you know that?"

"Oh, I hear the odd bit now and again."

She lay on her side, propping herself on one elbow.

My seemingly casual glance took in her jean clad legs and the light cotton shirt open at the throat. She was no longer the girl I remembered, but there was a sensual air about her, the aura of a mature woman aware of her power.

"Do you ever go back?" I asked. "I suppose you're too busy with your career."

"No. I don't go back. The lads go now and again."

"You travel around a good bit, I suppose," I offered.

"Umm. Always on the go. That's us."

"You've done very well. I have your records at home."

"A fan! That's nice."

I imagined that she was mocking me, like in the old days.

"No seriously, I think your stuff is terrific. Where did you learn to sing like that?"

"Oh, didn't you know? We always sang the old songs at home. The shee songs."

"The what?"

"The shee songs. You know. The little people, all that kind of stuff."

"Ah, I get it. The Sheehys. The gentry. That's very good." I laughed. "I remember how you used to kid me about all that."

"It's all true, you know," she smiled. "Nobody believes you when you tell the truth."

"Oh, I believe you all right. That's brilliant. The Sheehy Folk. I never thought of that." I nodded. "Newgrange and all that. Very good. You know I just missed you at Newgrange a couple of years ago. You were there the day before me."

"Is that so? We were just getting known at that time in Ireland. We were away for a few years."

"Aye," I said and waited.

"In America," she said, answering the unasked question. Suddenly she laughed.

"What's the joke?"

"Oh nothing. Just we thought we were a real Irish group, you know, the real thing."

"I'm sure you went down very well over there."

"Yes, except with an Irish group in Philadelphia. We performed at their St. Patrick's Day banquet and they eventually asked us politely to leave."

"Why was that?"

"They said we weren't Irish enough. They sent out for a proper Irish entertainer, someone who knew *Come into the Parlour* and so on." She laughed at the recollection.

"You can't win them all, can you?"

"I suppose not. Still we have one fan, I'm glad to hear."

She sat up and wrapped her arms about her knees, hugging herself as if for protection. The neck of her shirt gaped and I saw the swelling of her breast. She wore nothing under the shirt. There was a vertical line along the side of her breast suggesting that she had begun to sag slightly. I thought momentarily of toothless pigmy women with flaccid dangling pouches, while their younger sisters displayed their breasts with pride. I put the image from me.

"You look very strange," she said bringing me back with a jolt. "You still haven't told me about yourself."

"There's not much to tell. I have a good job and do quite nicely out of it."

"Is that all? You haven't got yourself married or anything?"

"Not even anything," I shrugged. "Never seemed to get the right opportunity."

"So what do you do with yourself?"

"Oh, I work fairly hard, you know." I frowned. There was very little to tell really. "Take the odd holiday and have the few jars." I said it casually, as if concealing the teeming multiplicity of my activities in a throwaway line, as one might wear dark glasses in the hope of being taken for a celebrity travelling incognito. "That's about it really." Who wants to hear about obsession, about a full and rewarding emotional life lived entirely in the mind? Could Mr O'Meara, just returned from the high intermontane plateaux of the Andes, convey to his listeners the bleak misery of the coca-chewing Indians and their hopeless pining for their lost Inca?

"Oh, I'd say you get about a bit. There was always a lot going on in that head of yours."

"I've always wondered about you," I said impulsively. "Ever since you-ah-went away."

She looked over at the child who was lying face down dabbling in the water.

"It's a long story."

"I have the time," I reassured her brightly. "I was always a good listener."

"True," she agreed and stared straight ahead.

I waited. Maybe the dam would burst after all this time and the old mystery would be solved. How had it all happened? Would her story lead at last to the body? Even the best detective has no case without the *corpus delicti*.

"Where's the stone?" she asked suddenly.

I put my hand into the pocket of my jacket, a good sensible Donegal tweed, with leather patches on the elbows. I felt the smooth pebble that I had carried with me for luck, down through all the years.

"Here it is," I said and placed it in her palm. "I always imagined it was a meteorite, for some reason."

She turned it in her palm and stroked the polished surface with her thumb.

"The tears of St. Lawrence," she murmured. "You see, I remember too."

And she told me then of the rows with her father; how he had wanted the hill even more than she had; how he had concluded the deal with Badger. She told me about John Olford too and how she had loved him literally to distraction. He would come down the hill in secret to meet her in the old fairy fort where they would lie together and make love, sometimes in the sunshine, and sometimes at night. Sometimes he free-wheeled his motor-bike down the hill and hid it in the woods and at other times he came across the swamp from their own place, clod-hopping as he called it and covered her body in wild, yellow swamp irises.

"I didn't like that," she said ruefully. "They were cold and made me think of lilies at a funeral. He had these gloomy moods sometimes."

I hung my head and fought the turmoil of emotion inside me.

"I can see you're embarrassed," she said sensing something of my upset, "but I did promise the whole story. He used to sit and look at me in the moonlight. I suppose he was a little bit mad but I would have done anything for him then."

"And then what happened? There was all sorts of talk, as you can guess." Me lu'd I submit that my client was unbearably provoked to a crime of passion. The jury followed my every word and gesture, mesmerised by the brilliance of my plea.

"Not very much really, in a sense. I got pregnant, *the* pregnant as Badger put it, making it sound like a disease. He still wanted to go through with the bargain, but I couldn't. John and I planned to run away." She stopped again and rubbed at her nose. "Itchy," she said, with an attempt at a smile. "That means you want a fight."

"Not with me I hope."

"No, no. I didn't want to go and yet I wanted it more than anything, if you follow me."

"And then?" I prompted gently.

"He pretended he was going to the Manx Grand Prix. That was to throw his family off the scent, and I was to meet him in London. He took his bike, of course. We were to go on to Australia together."

She exhaled slowly. "I think the idea of the baby frightened him. He never turned up. I waited a fortnight in this miserable hotel, till I ran out of money. Everyone was looking at me as if they knew all about me. I know they thought I was over there for an abortion. Maybe that was what he had in mind."

"And you never heard from him since?"

"Not a word. It's an old story, I suppose. I wouldn't be the first."

"The bastard." He deserved to be murdered. Exterminated like the rat he was. I had been instinctively right about him. A bomb plastique under the gold star on the petrol tank was what the great John Wahab deserved.

"I see. So that was the way it was." It explained everything.

"The da thought to patch things up with Badger, but I couldn't go through with it."

"And you had Ruth."

She picked at her finger nails. "Yes, I have Ruth."

I could think of nothing to say.

"I really believed him," she said after a while. She rocked slowly from side to side. "For a long time I hoped he would write. Maybe he did, but I never got any letters. I was in a home, you see and then after Ruth was born, I had a bit of a breakdown. There's a name for it."

"I know," I nodded not wishing to speak of the devil.

"I was in the looney-bin," she said with a brittle laugh, looking directly at me. "Can you believe that?"

"Oh Kate," I said, fighting a painful constriction of the throat, "I had no idea." My eyes prickled with tears. I put my hands on her shoulders and drew her towards me.

"You needn't worry," she said with an attempt at a laugh "I'm not dangerous." Her voice was muffled by the Donegal tweed and I felt the tension gradually ebbing from her. I stroked her hair and her cheek and felt tears on my fingers.

"It's o.k." I said. "It's o.k. now." It reminded me of another time.

"What are you doing to her?" said the child standing over me accusingly. "Mammy never cries".

"It's o.k." I said again like a cracked record, "we were just talking about the old days."

A chill wind riffled the surface of the lake, shattering the dark image of the mountain. White cats' paws darted about. For the first time I wondered why she was there and realised that it was almost dusk.

They were staying in the cottage among the trees at the far end of the lake. Apparently they sometimes rented it to work in peace and seclusion.

"You can stay the night if you like," she offered, dabbing at her eyes. "It's a long way into town. The lads would be glad to see you."

"I really should be back at work tomorrow morning early," I said dubiously.

"Mitch," she said impishly with a gleam of her old humour.

"You got me into trouble over that before, if I recall correctly."

She laughed aloud. "Just a little mini-mitch," she said, "just for old time's sake."

She nudged against me and I felt the softness of her body.

"O.K." I agreed and resolved to develop a more suave line of conversation. "I just hope the mammy doesn't find out this time."

She hooked her arm through mine in the way that I remembered and walked me towards the crushed granite track while the little girl ran on ahead.

The low sun crept from behind the shoulder of the mountain casting a soft green light around the stand of pine trees. It was almost like coming home.

I drove slowly along the mountain road with the windows down. Fitful sunlight chased the cloud shadows through the valley below, Glenasmole where Oisin fell off his horse after his return from the land of the Ever Young. It behoved me to go carefully. *Terre verte* and brown, the valley was camouflaged in the colours of the model aeroplanes that used to hang from our bedroom ceilings. Hurricanes,

Messerschmitts and Lancasters and, supreme among them, the Spitfire, they swirled in a crazy dogfight whenever the door or window was opened.

Bandit at nine o'clock, said a warning voice in my brain. Not ten feet from the car, riding the thermal with the grace and arrogance of a fighter ace, was a kestrel. He looked at me with one glittering onyx eye, gave a little left rudder, a touch of aileron and peeled off from the formation to dive away into the valley. I raised my hand to salute as he dwindled to a speck and vanished from my sight.

Seventeen

"Do you know what she reminded me of?" asked Anto, cutting his steak into regular cubes. He speared a segment and paused, holding it halfway to his mouth. Around us was the hum of the late night city and from the tiny kitchen, the clatter of dishes.

"You're going to tell us anyway," smiled Jean tolerantly. "I hope he won't disillusion you about your lady friend, Jamie."

"She's not my lady friend, as you put it," I replied quickly, although I was pleased at the assumption.

A svelte young waitress appeared beside us.

"Would madam care for some more vegetables?" she intoned.

Anto indicated his plate and she moved around to unload a pile of assorted vegetables onto the little space that was left. I could see how the waitress responded to him without a word being spoken. I apparently did not register and she vanished backwards through the swing doors into the rackety steam of the kitchen.

At the table behind us a middle-aged man and a tall young woman were engaged in an argument in low venomous tones of quite chilling ferocity.

"There's no need to take that attitude," he kept repeating like a refrain. Anto swallowed and returned to his theme.

"She reminds me of a kind of a sexy Mother Machree."

I laughed. He had put his finger on the effect Kate's act had on me. Jean instinctively patted the back of my hand. She assumed already that I had some kind of proprietorial claim on Kate.

"I think she's a terrific performer," she asserted stoutly.

"That's it," Anto pounced on the word. "She's a performer. She really slays an audience."

"There's no doubt about that," I agreed. I had never seen her perform in public before and was impressed by her mastery over the audience. She ran the whole gamut of emotions, at times plaintive and vulnerable and at other times positively raunchy. They loved her. A man in front of me stood and shouted *bravo* after the final number. I envied him his self-confidence. There are people who can say 'hear, hear', in loud tones at lectures and give the impression that they know more than the rest of us. *Bravo* spoke more of La Scala than The Holy Ground and put the rest of us in our place. I applauded enthusiastically but I could not quite buy the whole performance.

"What did you think of it though?" I pressed him.

"Magic," he declared. "Hard to believe they're the same snot-nosed brats we used to chase out of the station."

"I did all the bloody stock-taking," snarled the young woman at the other table. "I stayed up all bloody night to do it and see what I get."

"Keep your voice down," pleaded her companion, looking around in furtive agony.

The waitress appeared again, deferred to Anto and went off to get some more wine. I twirled the stem of my glass and drank sparingly. Like everyone else, they saw the public side of Kate. I felt a bit superior, privileged and a trifle cynical. Maybe I was jealous of her and wanted to take her down a peg or two. Perhaps I felt that the audience would always be there to take her away from me. I had no claim on her anyway.

"There's a big price differential on parts between here and the North," said the man, employing a diversionary tactic with no success. The young woman began to sob. Tears ran down her cheeks and dropped onto her plate.

"I'll bet you wouldn't bring your bloody wife out and ask her to eat in the kitchen." She dabbed at her eyes with her napkin.

"There's no need to take that attitude," he said again in despair, like a punter who clings to his cherished system although bankruptcy is staring him in the face.

Anto gave us a conspiratorial roll of the eyes and tackled his plate. A police siren wailed through the night, the noise rising as it got closer and dwindling to the vaguest memory of an echo.

"I hate that sound," said Jean, with a slight shiver. "I always try to imagine what they're going to find when they get there."

"That's a sombre thought," I said, "though, God knows, you hear enough of them nowadays. Things have changed." It was a favourite theme of mine, security grids on shops in what used to be a strollers' city. "There was a time when you could walk the streets without meeting gangs of young gurriers."

"The sons of Belial," declaimed Anto, "then wander forth the sons of Belial, flown with insolence and wine."

"Thank you, professor," said Jean smiling and I could sense the affection between them.

"It's a fact though. Things have gone to the dogs."

"What do you blame for that? When did it all start to go haywire?" Anto came highly recommended by Mr. O'Meara and I was interested in his opinion. He shoved his fork into a pile of french fried onions. "I think the country started to go down the drain in the sixties when they started servin' these yokes instead of good Catholic, Irish, fried onions. Jesus Christ," he said with theatrical passion, "it's like eatin' cardboard, fuckin' curtain rings."

He put the lot into his mouth and munched away.

"Ssh," admonished his wife and he looked aggrieved.

The couple at the other table suspended hostilities and looked around. Anto shrugged, by way of apology.

"Well, it is," he repeated. "But seriously, ten, fifteen years ago we hadn't arses in our trousers and now everybody goes on about where you can get a good meal for what some people would be lucky to earn in a week. Far from it we were reared."

"What about the North?" said Jean seriously. "Don't you think the whole business has brutalised everyone?" She leaned her elbows on the table. I watched them with a twinge of envy. They were absorbed in their discussion and in each other. I thought of Sinatra's Chicago, 'I saw a man and he danced with his wife'. I felt not so much *El Gavilan*, the hawk, circling and observing, but rather like a dishevelled jackdaw, hopping around the periphery of the discussion, picking up the crumbs.

"When Garda Fallon was murdered, everybody looked the other way," said Jean. "If you want to name the day that things started to go wrong, that's the one." Anto frowned. He pushed the remnants of his meal around and sat up straight. He rubbed his chin thoughtfully.

"She's right, you know. Begod, this is a very serious discussion."

He cast around for the waitress and she materialised beside him.

"Certainly sir," she nodded. "No trouble at all."

"A bang o' the latch," he explained as she backed away through the swing doors, which swung behind her. In a sudden lull her voice carried clearly: "Jaysus, I'm dyin' for a lash."

The sombre mood lifted and we collapsed around the table. The young woman stood up in fury and threw down her napkin.

"And you needn't think you can get your typing done on the side either," she accused and started for the door. Her companion lumbered after her, perspiring and rooting for his wallet.

"That's a new angle on it, anyway," observed Anto. The waitress, elegant and deferential, appeared with a tray of drinks and smiled upon us.

"I didn't know they'd moved it," he mused as if to himself.

It was a mild night with just the suggestion of an autumnal dew. I locked the car and stretched, breathing in the scent of growing things. I was reluctant to go indoors and thought of my brother and his wife. I knew that Jean would drive home. Anto is not a great driver, but he is an even worse passenger, except when he has had a few. They would be all right, I reflected. I laughed to myself, recollecting his yarn about our father, the old man, as he had come to be called, and how he had secreted half a mixed grill in his pockets to avoid offending his host. That was in the days when weddings took place in the morning and the last survivors were hungry again by ten o'clock at night.

He had quailed at the size of the meal in front of him and through the fumes of a serious day's drinking, had hit on the plan of slipping the components in to his handkerchief and distributing them, Houdini-like, about his person. All was revealed when he opened his wallet and tried to pay for a round of drinks with a couple of lean back rashers. I chuckled aloud. I heard the click of a car door and my heart jumped.

"The first sign of madness, talking to yourself."

"Jesus, you put the heart across me," I said as Kate stepped into the light. "What are you doing here?"

"I just felt like dropping in." She looked around. "So this is where you hang out."

"You'd better come inside," I said, fumbling with my keys. Into my parlour, said the spider to the fly. My fingers mutinied and the keys fell to the ground.

"Out on the tiles, I'll bet," she mocked.

I found the right key at last and opened the door to the lobby.

"What are the neighbours like?" she asked in a stage whisper.

"I never see them," I replied.

The lift purred upwards and we stepped into the darkened flat. Kate went to the window and pulled back the curtain. A dim light crept into the room.

"What's that building over there?" she asked, indicating the dark bulk of the convent across the park.

Standing behind her I could smell the perfume of her hair. I could feel my pulse pounding.

"The convent," I said, swallowing. "That light patch is the nuns' graveyard." She gave a little shiver and moved against me.

"A cheerful prospect," she remarked as I slipped my arms around her. She turned slowly and raised her face to me. I felt the wetness of her lips and the warmth of her body as she strained against me. A surge of power went through me and I was omnipotent.

Suddenly we were on the floor, tearing at each other with a savage urgency until we lay satiated and naked together in the half light. Puddles of clothing lay about the room. She raised herself Sphinx like on her elbows and lay half across me so that her nipples brushed the hair on my chest. I need not have worried on that score. She followed my downward glance.

"Do you remember the first time you touched my breasts?"

"The only time," I pointed out. "I didn't think you even knew."

"Dirty little bleeder," she laughed and her teeth gleamed whitely. Her hair cascaded about her face and shoulders.

"It's probably no harm to mention at this point, that I've been madly in love with you since as long back as I can remember. Just for the record."

"Very polite of you to mention it," she said primly, "now that we've got acquainted again.'"

She made no reciprocal declaration and I felt a stab of panic, a feeling that perhaps I was just one of many, someone to supply a momentary need, even another scalp for a collection. For the moment I was happy enough not to know. Her fingers idly traced the line of my mouth.

"You're frowning," she challenged.

"Just remembering," I said as lightly as possible.

"Do you know what I'd like now more than anything?" She laid her head on my chest.

"What?" Thinks: can I rise to the occasion? The cartoon thought bubbles floated overhead.

"A cup of coffee and a sandwich."

"A cup of coffee and a sandwich!"

"And a sandwich," she insisted.

"Would cheese be romantic enough? I might have a bit of ham."

"Cheese would be fine, with a bit of mustard."

She rolled away and reached for her blouse. I retrieved my trousers and headed for the kitchen. When I returned the room had brightened perceptibly. She was curled up on the couch with a blanket wrapped around her.

"What are you walking like that for?" she asked and I realised that I was bent double, as if there were snipers outside the window.

"The nuns," I replied sheepishly. "They could see in."

She laughed aloud. "Not even nuns have eyesight that good. Here," she added, lifting the edge of the blanket, "get in and keep warm."

She wolfed the sandwich and sipped slowly at the coffee. I slipped in beside her although I was forced to keep one foot on the floor, like the Hays office stipulation. Gradually a warm, contented lassitude crept over me.

"You know, you really are a bit mad," I murmured after some time.

"On the contrary," said Kate. "I'm one of the few people with papers to prove that I'm sane. Can you say as much?"

"No, I suppose not."

My right arm was beginning to go numb but I was prepared to make the sacrifice, even unto gangrene if necessary. People rarely mean it literally when they use the expression.

More light filtered into the room and the trees in the park began to appear against a pale ribbon of lemon coloured sky.

"What's that?" asked Kate drowsily and I saw that she was looking at the panel on the wall. She sat up and blood began to force its way into my atrophied veins. Pins and needles invaded the limb urging me to irrational laughter.

"Aah," I said foolishly, flexing the mangled limb.

"Just a model I made up years ago with fibre-glass and that. It's Brehonys' Hill actually."

I waited, watching with certain apprehension to see her reaction. She climbed over me, clad only in her blouse and stood unselfconsciously in front of the map. She touched the hill tentatively and ran her finger down the line of the stream to where it lost itself in the swamp. I watched fascinated until I thought once more of the nuns, then rolled off the couch and grabbed at the curtains. If the nuns had zoom lenses, I was in trouble.

"I'd like to go and see it again," she said slowly.

I switched on an amber spotlight and evening shadows fell across the land, reaching out from the line of wood and highlighting the little roundel fort on the hill. The light spilled over her skin giving her a Polynesian glow.

"Will you take me there now, Jamie?"

"What now?" I yawned, subtly conveying the impression that bed would be a better idea.

"I want to go now," she insisted. "We can come back here later."

"Look," I said gently, "it's not there anymore. I told you they dug it all away for gravel years ago. I told you that, didn't I, that day, down at the lake?" She hung her head and I said gently:

"I could show you where it is now, if you like."

That was a stupid suggestion at the time, but she nodded.

"All right. Show me." She began to pluck at her buttons.

The tyres made an insistent tearing sound on the ribbed concrete as I drove through the deserted streets. There is a certain pleasure in driving through the city in the very early morning, without the fear of other irate road-users. A tinkers' pony, ghostly white in the pale light, trotted across the road on twisted, unshod hooves. We passed an open space with goalposts and a burnt out car, a recreational area. There were rows of identical pale yellow houses with low pitched roofs. There were shops, closed like metal boxes, with bollards in front of the windows.

"They lost a couple of builders in there," I said flippantly. "The council sent in a search party but they never found hide or hair of them."

She gave a bleak smile. "It looks a bit grim, doesn't it?"

"Readymade for urban guerrillas," I suggested.

"Who could blame them. Did you have a hand in this?" It was like an accusation.

"God, no. I'm not that bad. No, but my partner redesigned an old country pub. The owner is the local politician and gombeen man. He wanted the whole works."

"The whole works?"

"Yeah, traditional stuff, as he said himself. Plenty of Howth stone and fibre-glass roofbeams. Cartwheels set into the windows and cabaret every weekend."

I turned into a large empty parking lot. Before us stood The Rainbow's End, a vast square monstrosity complete with an illuminated plastic sign showing a leprechaun with his crock of gold.

"Traditional," I said wryly. "Country and western and moneylenders."

"The Rainbow's End," she repeated softly. "I think I want to go home now." She put her head back on the head rest and closed her eyes.

I drove slowly, not sure where she wanted to go. A squad car moved in behind me and followed for a while. When it pulled out to pass I saw the white faces of two young policemen as they looked closely at us. They were tired and coming to the end of their shift. I wondered what random dangers they had encountered in the darkness, or whether they had passed a night of total boredom.

I had almost to carry Kate from the car and got her into my bed with some difficulty. Against my finer instincts I showered and went to work. When I came back her car was gone. There was a note sellotaped to Brehonys' Hill. It said 'Ring me' and included a 'phone number. I felt relief flooding through my mind and put the note carefully into my wallet. By now she was most likely on stage again.

Anto rang.

"You got home all right?"

"No bother. Jean did the driving, which was just as well. We were stopped by the Guards."

"Could've been awkward."

"'Have you been drinking, mam?' says he to Jean. 'Just one or two,' says your woman. 'That's not very wise now, is it mam?' says he. 'Well,' says she, looking over at meself, 'have you considered the alternative?'"

"What did he say to that?"

"Ah, he just laughed. 'I take your point,' says he and waves us on." I laughed. "The luck of the devil."

"It was a very enjoyable evening though, all the same. It was very decent of you to organise it."

"Well, I knew you'd be interested."

"And what about yourself?"

"How do you mean?"

"Ah nothin' really. Just Jean felt a bit down, when she saw you headin' off by yourself, you know; back to the oul' flat, and that."

"Ah, sure we all have our cross to carry."

I was touched, but could not help a secret grin. "Tell Jean not to worry about me. I'm fine."

"Anyway, lookit, don't be a stranger as they say. I told her you were too damn smart to get yourself lumbered."

"You never know. Stranger things have happened."

"I dare say. I'll believe it when I see it."

He rang off, leaving me feeling quite smug. I tried the television. A well known celebrity was interviewing another well known celebrity. I went back to my drawing board. We often say that to express a sense of spectacular failure, but with me it was the reverse. I relaxed in the security of set square and T square. Perched in the monastic circle of light from my anglepoise, I worked far into the night.

She told me they were going to Australia for a few months. Apparently it was a great opportunity. A black fear descended on me. I had known it all along.

"Don't look so glum," she said. "It's only for a few months."

"And what am I to do?" I asked feeling like a child.

"Oh, I know you," she teased. "You'll find plenty of company. I've no doubt."

"That's not true," I sulked. "Whether you believe it or not, I've always been faithful to you over the years." I was a picture of injured innocence.

"In your fashion, as they say."

I shrugged. "Well I never even knew where you were."

"Don't worry. I'm not the jealous type."

"Well, I am," I said. "My imagination works overtime."

"I always thought you were the logical type."

I was silent for a while, drumming my fingers on the dashboard. I knew that he was in Australia. I knew for certain that she would see him and that would be the end for me. To hell with her, I thought. I'm not going to be made a fool of.

"He's over there, isn't he?" I might as well say it as think it.

She flinched. "He wouldn't mean anything to me now, if you mean John Olford. That all died on me years ago."

"I'm sorry. I shouldn't have brought that up."

"It doesn't matter. I don't mind talking about it now. It's like talking about a stranger."

I was still not reassured. I could see him, with his supercilious half grin and I knew that I could never match him. By now he would be a mature man in the prime of his life, with the additional insouciance of the stereotyped Australian. I saw him beating the dust of the outback from his bush-shirt and sweeping her into his muscular sun-tanned arms. Not for the first time, I wished that the rumours about Badger might have proved true.

"You needn't worry," she said gently, taking my hand. "I had all that knocked out of me with E.C.T."

"Oh Christ," I said, "I never realised."

"It's a bit like fixing the radio with a bang of the poker," she said with a dismissive laugh. "They took me apart and put me back together in the hospital."

"Every time my old man did that with anything, he always had a few bits left over," I could have bitten my tongue off when I had said it.

"You're probably right," she replied drily. "Anyway that's one bit that must have been left out."

I wanted to believe her. I wanted to tell her to go to Hell.

"Will I see you before I go?" she asked with a slight tremor in her voice.

"What's wrong with tonight?"

"Not a thing," she said and smiled her old dazzling smile that captivated me and swept aside all argument. For better or for worse, I was still under the spell.

Eighteen

Winter is the time for introspection. I went home to my parents' house for Christmas. I walked by myself, along by the sea, looking I imagined like one of those gloomy types in the French art films: a small figure in the distance on a wet beach, a speck of human significance on a great wet smear of lead coloured sand; a haunting theme emphasising the loneliness, a close-up of the face haunted by suffering, eyes sunken with weariness and pain. Grey water tumbled at my feet. The pebbles seethed in the undertow and large stones jarred. In my mind constantly was a vision of a vehicle, a utility I believe they call them out there, blurred and shimmering on a stave of mirage, floating on the heat haze, always approaching out of the Never-Never, out of the Dreamtime. Inexorably it came on, my death-coach, until I could see the 'roo bars on the front, 'roo bars, a joke, a macho affectation that crushes bone and flesh and casts them to one side.

She would smile then and climb aboard and that would be the end for me. I thought of her, wooing her audiences on the far side of the globe. They would fall for her act as everyone did, except me. I was not one of her constituents. I was wise to her. They would laugh together again and laugh about me and all the years would be swept aside. Well, to hell with her.

I walked out along the railway in dark depression. A few black and wizened leaves clung here and there in the hedgerows. The hill was gone, except for the very edge that stuck up all around like the rim of a lunar crater. A bulldozer drove back and forth over acres of garbage, like a giant bed mite rooting. Plastic bags splayed against the tall wire mesh fencing, like failed escapees from some terrible death camp. I went closer. The bulldozer surfed on a wave of indescribable filth, the detritus of urban civilization. A black lake lurked in a hollow near where I imagined the old house to have stood. Oil glistened on the surface and a stench like tom-cats rose from it. 'All finished now', whispered the ice to my inner ear. It was all gone. The stream had sagged into a deep straight trench that cut right through the swamp. The swamp itself was gone.

Green shoots of winter wheat stretched like a fabric over what had once been wetland. The soil looked hard and stony from deep ploughing. The trench sucked the water from the land and to my professional eye, the ground seemed lower in relation to the line of the railway. Of course, like a dried loofah, it had shrunk as the water oozed into the arterial drain. I saw no frogs or geese and, by the grey turgid waters of Brehonys' Bottoms, I sat down and wept.

The telephone jangled in the darkness and I heard my father shuffling in the hallway. In Pavlovian manner he still reacted to bells and signals.

"Bloody Hell," he grumbled and the ringing stopped. I heard some further mumbling.

"It's five in the morning," he expostulated and then he shouted up to me that someone claiming to be in Australia wanted to speak to me.

"Merry bloody Christmas," he growled as I grabbed the receiver from him. "Very bloody funny I must say."

He shuffled away into the kitchen, scratching himself and clutching his pyjamas. His generation, I noted, were all impervious to the cold of early morning lino. Kate's voice crackled from the other side of the world.

"Merry Christmas," she shouted.

"Hey. It's all right, I can hear you perfectly. Merry Christmas to you too. It's great to hear from you. Where are you? What are you doing?"

My father's head appeared around the kitchen door. He informed me that the kettle was on. He hesitated for a moment and withdrew, leaving the door ajar.

They were having their Christmas dinner, sitting outside in the sunshine.

"Who's there?" I asked immediately, suspicion surging through me. This was some elaborate joke.

"Just ourselves," she replied and I sensed something unsaid. "We were feeling lonely. It can get very boring at times."

"It's five in the morning here." I offered this piece of information and then thought it sounded like a complaint. "Not that I'm complaining."

The head came round the door again. "Two sugars?"

I nodded rather impatiently and the head withdrew.

"It's great to hear from you," I repeated. "Is everything going well?"

"Fine, fine," she said. "I had a great idea. I want you to design a house for me." Pip, pip, pip

"A house?" I said urgently.

"We'll need some sort of a house when we get married, won't we?" Pip, p-i-i-p. The line went dead. I looked at the receiver and rattled the phone cradle, as people always do, always to no avail.

"Your coffee's ready." I saw the look of comic surprise on his face as he caught me in the middle of a leap of silent exultation, fists clenched and punching the air.

"Seein' as how it's Christmas, I put a little nip into it. Good news, I take it?" he added seeing my broad grin.

"Not bad, not bad," I conceded, "a commission from a client in Australia."

"Hmmh," he grunted. "The electric fire is on, if you want to drink that in the kitchen. Funny bloody time to ring up about it." He shook his head. "Anyway a happy Christmas, Jamie. I think I'll toddle back to bed."

"Hold on a minute. There's something else."

"I might have guessed."

He sat down in front of the fire and lifted his bare feet to the warmth.

"Might as well put on another bar."

"I think I'm going to get married," I said, holding the mug in both hands. There was a fair old belt of whiskey in it.

"Heh, heh," he chuckled "you think you're going to get married. Anyone in particular?"

"Yes, as a matter of fact. Do you remember Kate Sheehy? Dan Sheehy's daughter." He took a long pull at his coffee and sat back on the hard kitchen chair.

"Well, I'll be damned. Dan Sheehy's daughter? The little wild one with the red hair?" He rubbed the grey stubble on his chin. "Well, I'll be damned. Is that who was on the phone?"

"That's right. She's in Australia."

"There was a noticeable absence of endearments."

"Not my style, I suppose."

"No, I suppose not." He exhaled slowly and his breath drifted in a little plume in the chilly air. I thought I saw a tear form in the corner of his eye but with the old it is often difficult to tell.

"They were the best days, Jamie, when you were all youngsters. Do you remember?"

"Aye."

"The fire in the oul' signal box. Things to do all day long. Sure there's nobody to talk to nowadays. I've buried most of my old customers. Do you remember the way I used to kid you about the fairies?"

"I kind of half believed you then."

"That's all gone now."

"Not all of it. There's still a little bit of the magic left."

The whiskey was making us maudlin.

"The magic, aye. I wonder though, what your mother will have to say. You were always the white-headed boy."

I felt a twinge of the old guilt. The title was undeserved. Anto and his family looked after them year in, year out, but I always got the credit.

"A sad old business," he began again. "And tell me, how did things turn out for her?"

I told him as much as he needed to know and his sympathetic nature responded to the story of a child distressed and betrayed by a scoundrel. I said nothing of my own fear. The fish was on the line but there was a way to go before she was landed.

"The bowsie. Poor Badger was right. The old man sold up after all that, and went back to England."

"How do you mean, *back* to England? Weren't they here for the last three hundred years, and their Barnwell relations before them?"

"Ah, you know what I mean. They never really settled here. They were always English in their own mind. English schools, British army, that kind of thing."

"Right enough," I nodded thoughtfully.

"Funny though," he went on. "I sort of miss him around. I always used to wonder about him. It's all bungalows up there now with porticoes and colonnades and stuff. You'd be interested in them." He chuckled. "There's even a fella with a plastic brushwood fence, all jaggedy bits, all the same." He laughed aloud. "I don't know. Tell you what, we'll have another of these, seein' the day that's in it and that'll put us in nice fettle for early mass." I felt the warm routine of home close around me and I stretched my feet out to the heat.

"Well, you'll give the tongues something to wag about anyway," said my mother when she came down to investigate, "Kate Sheehy." She pursed her lips and went to rattle the kettle. "I wondered what all the noise was about."

There was a long silence as she shuffled about, getting some breakfast.

"You can't go to Communion now," she accused, "not with that whiskey inside you."

We hung our heads.

"Well you're a grown man, Jamie. I presume you know what you're doing."

There is a widespread belief about the age of reason (and of criminal responsiblity) being seven, contrary to all the evidence. The position of grown-up is foisted on people totally unqualified for the job. Seniority is the only criterion.

"Jamie has put me in the picture," said my father. "There was a lot of misunderstanding about that business." Bacon sizzled. "You might as well have a fry," she declared "seein' as how you're not going to the altar."

She grunted some more, turning things over in her mind and in the pan, a non-stick job scratched beyond redemption with a metal spatula. "It must be the Brehony drop in you," she said caustically. "They were never too bright."

"Well now, if you think about it, maybe it's the way things were meant to work out." I had never thought of the Brehony drop in me until that moment. "Haven't they lived side by side for thousands of years. Maybe it's time we got together." There was a poetic rightness to it all.

"Don't take me for a fool. We're not in a story-book, you know."

She fished out a couple of fried eggs and I realised that I was starving. Small shreds of Teflon adhered to them.

"There were always two kinds of Brehonys, the mad ones and the grand ones. I always thought you had a touch of the grandeur. Your brother Anthony of course is one of the other kind."

I was not too sure if she intended it as a compliment to me.

"Well," said my father, reaching for a plate, "at least you won't be saying that he was too near to get married."

"What do you mean 'near'?"

For a moment he was confused.

"Ah nothing. We just wondered sometimes if you were a bit too eh, self-centred to notice anyone else, let alone, fall for someone."

"You meant 'mean', didn't you?"

For a moment the injustice of it hurt. I was never mean. At least, if I was told about someone in need, I was never mean. Always bought my round.

"No, no," he protested, "we never meant that. It's just you were always, sort of, self-contained. We used to worry that you would be left on your own." So, like Anto and Jean, they had worried too. Frankly, I was puzzled. How could someone who nurtured a burning love all his life, ever be considered cold, or selfish? Surely it was obvious to everyone that the whole world was encompassed by my goodwill towards all. I had to laugh. I had presents for all of my brother's children enough to shatter the peace of a Christmas afternoon. I even remembered their names. It was obviously a case of mistaken identity.

"Well, anyway. That's the holy all of it," I said without rancour. "You needn't worry about having to receive Dan Sheehy, if that's what's on your mind. They haven't spoken for years." I might have sounded a bit harsh. My mother sniffed. "Don't think I'm a snob. I've nothing against the poor man. I'm only concerned for your happiness."

I felt rebuked. "Don't worry on that score," I assured her and she gave a flicker of a smile.

"These rashers are very tender," said my father, patting the back of her hand. "Very tender indeed."

"Not legal tender, though," I reminded him and they laughed.

The awkwardness was at an end and we relaxed to enjoy Christmas.

I wondered about the mad Brehony drop. I began to work on the house.

I waited for her letters and wrote back in high excitement. People remarked on the change in me. She told me when to expect her home.

I planned a house for us. It had walls, a roof, various rooms and all the usual fittings such as windows and doors, but it was not right. I planned an alternative, a Frank Lloyd Wright job, a filing cabinet clinging to a cliff face, some drawers open, some half closed, balconies and terraces, but vertigo got to me just looking at the sketch.

I looked at old Georgian houses where the floor boards played host to every species of fungus and woodworm and my heart sank with the joists. I toyed with wigwams and ziggurats, New Mexican ranch-style bungalows and classical villas, but gradually I began to clarify where I wanted to live. Like the Brehonys before me, I would build on a hill, partly under the ground. I had adopted retroactively, those old misty figures from the past. It had always been our way to live close to the earth. My family tree reached back to the Brennus and his contempt for urban living. I sketched away, the idea taking form on the drawing board as the reasons clarified themselves in my imagination.

I sank a hollow into a hilltop and built my house downwards. The main windows opened onto the east, south and west, while the restored line of the hill flowed over the roof. Oblique shafts, Corbusier-like, conducted the sunlight to all parts of my house. Solar panels on the hillside soaked up the sunlight and brought heat through serpentine pipes, to every corner. The grain of the timber casing was fossilised in the concrete for ever more. Coccooned in vis-queen and insulation we could live snugly with spectacular views. The roof of grass and shrubs would never blow off.

But what about planning permission? Because it would merge with the landscape, because it was not an eyesore, it would surely be turned down. Regretfully I put it aside, as another of my dreams. *Lucerna* the lantern, I thought of it. It would never be built. And yet, wherever I went I looked for a suitable hill that I could buy. My ancestors were never so diffident. Could I slay the entire staff of the council planning department?

On a bright dry morning, my car was covered with dust. A bubble of high-pressure pushing upwards from the Mediterranean, unusual for the time of year, carried fine dust in the upper atmosphere and part of the Sahara descended on my new car. The roof was stippled with a fine reddish film. It excited comment and disbelief in the evening papers, but I knew it was no exaggeration. Freak weather conditions or not, the Sahara was spreading. African countries were being racked by famine while their thuggish dictators conducted genocidal wars or spirited the country's reserves to convenient Swiss banks. Collection boxes rattled in Grafton Street and we bought our consciences off with a few bob. The dust was an unwelcome reminder of a continent withering. I washed the car.

I looked at pictures of famine. Biafra was one thing. It had been man made;famine as an instrument of policy, but this was different. Here the land itself was blowing away, whirling in the upper atmosphere, lofted by the jet streams. These child-skeletons were not a political ploy. This was the inexorable march of desert. Like my childhood fear of the Mau Mau, I saw the desert advancing out of the south, searing all before it until the whole planet became like an anvil for the sun. The apocalyptic vision was too much for me. I am no Hieronymus Bosch. I got out the turtle-wax and gave the car a good shine. From nowhere at all, Mr O'Meara came into my mind. He had the answer in his back garden.

The idea seized on me. I put house plans aside and immersed myself, figuratively, in a desalination plant. The Rain House gradually took shape, tall and angular but with something of the atmosphere of the Victorian palm house. I read up about solar-powered refrigeration. It was as beautifully simple as the perpetual motion machine: salt water in, evaporation under the intense tropical sun, condensation on the refrigerated panels pendant from the roof like punkahs or battle flags in some old cathedral, and out flowed the life-giving clear, fresh water. Capital intensive, I admit, but cheaper than a M.I.G. fighter or a ground to air missile. I sent photo-copies to Mr O'Meara who replied with enthusiasm. Nobody else to whom I sent copies replied. The desert is still spreading.

By visualising the thing and by drawing it out, I felt that to some degree I had made it work. I warned myself against, becoming an eccentric like Mr O'Meara. One obsession per lifetime is enough for anyone.

The doorbell rang and, tall and tanned with sun-bleached wisps in her hair, my obsession was standing there.

"I didn't expect you for a few weeks more," I said, at a bit of a loss, still thinking about guttering and storage systems.

"I couldn't stand the strine," she smiled and I wondered at first, if she had acquired an accent.

"Oh, yeh, I get it."

"You could say you were glad to see me," she said, cocking her head quizzically to one side.

"You have no idea," I said and my voice shook. "It's so good to see you again." So he never materialised after all. I was safe. We held each other and I felt happiness coursing through my veins like a strong cordial. We recognised our urgent need for each other and I drew her inside and closed the door.

Nineteen

"I know you've been wondering," she said one day, "if I heard anything from John Olford when we were out there."

"It might have crossed my mind once or twice," I lied offhand.

We were lying in bed on a Sunday morning with the curtains drawn back to admit the sun. I had been conducting a furtive pursuit of crumbs of toast that had turned my side of the bed into a fakir's couch.

"We didn't exactly make headline news, you know. It wasn't as if the entire population of Australia was all agog with excitement."

"So you didn't hear from him after all. Ah well."

"No, not a word. I hope you'll believe me when I say I'm glad too. No point in opening old sores."

"I suppose not."

I looked her straight in the eye. There was no duplicity there.

"I love you, Jamie," she said, for the first time that I could ever recall. "Maybe I always did, but you were such a solemn little boy."

"Huh."

"I always thought you were such a kind and sensitive little chap though."

"Not so much of the little. Incidentally my parents think I'm a bit of a cold fish, a bit of a tight wad actually."

I was trawling for compliments.

"Supposing I told them what a violent and passionate lover you are," she teased, running her finger down my chest, dislodging even more small shards of toast. "You're a messy eater though."

Her thigh moved against mine.

"Why are we getting married, by the way?" she asked after a

moment of tense speculative silence. "Haven't we all the comforts of home as we are?"

"It was your idea, wasn't it. I've been trying to ask you for the past twenty years, but you wouldn't listen to me."

My hand cupped the warm soft roundness of her breast.

"Twenty years, man and boy. It beats *the Dancing Girls of Kush*." I smiled to myself.

"What's that about dancing girls?" She reared up on her elbow and I gazed at her light skinned nakedness.

"Just an old *National Geographic*", I said, laughing and explained the joke.

"I always said you were a dirty-minded little bleeder," she scolded and rolled on top of me. "Do you want me to close the curtains?"

"Forget the nuns," I said with masterly decisiveness, "I'm more worried about those crumbs."

Another time she leafed through drawings that were scattered around the flat. I am as firm a believer in system as my friend, Howie, is in monogamy, and one of these days I intend to try it, system that is. System makes the universe work, but in evolutionary terms my filing has reached the stage of primordial chaos. A room accommodates my ideas, finished work, work in progress and ideas still-born after a couple of tentative strokes. Blue prints pile up on the floor or stand in clusters of cylinders like stunted church organs. But everything I need is there somewhere. A space to work in is all I crave.

"What's this?" she asked and I explained about the rain house.

"It works," I insisted. "I've seen the prototype."

I told her about Mr O'Meara's plan and his garden cloche. Unexpectedly she was moved by the story.

"If only more people thought like that. It would be a better world."

"But he's a total pessimist. That's the funny part of it."

"You're not a pessimist though, are you?"

"I hope I'm an optimist, at least."

"I like the way you worry about things in general. Are you, by the way, a religious person? I often wondered."

"Not so's you'd notice, I go in more for hope than for faith, as I've probably said before."

She looked at the diagram. "It makes a certain amount of sense."

She sat cross-legged among the papers. "Interesting," she murmured.

"Have you finished my house yet?"

"There's dozens of them there," I said, indicating a stack. "Have a look for yourself. I can offer you the whole works and convert your garage as an extra bonus."

I left her to it for a while and went back to my work. My pencil scratched loudly in the quiet of the room. Paper rustled. I became absorbed in a problem involving conversion from feet to metres, something that still gives me trouble, just as the non-native speaker is never truly at home in his adopted language. A six foot-six policeman has both a physical and psychological edge on a two metres tall criminal. My local pub experimented with half litres for a while, but the stuff never tasted quite the same.

"What's this?" She interrupted my train of thought. I had had no intention of showing her my hill-top house. That was my own private dream. I like to think that I present a commonsense, practical exterior to my potential customers.

"Ah, just a flight of fancy, if that's not a contradiction in terms."

She held up the tracing and the light from the anglepoise shone through it, giving it the opaque glow of old parchment. The drawing stood out sharply. I watched her as she studied the drawing slowly, sometimes following a line with her finger or turning the floor plan through one hundred and eighty degrees as if to visualise the rooms from every angle.

"Can it be done?" she asked after a while.

"I honestly don't know. Anyway you'd have a lot of trouble finding a site."

"I suppose. I like the idea though."

"I don't know if it's reassuring to find that one of us is as daft as the other."

"If it worked it wouldn't be daft, would it?"

"No, I suppose it wouldn't."

"Well, think about it."

We left it at that but the idea kept returning to me at odd hours, sometimes coming between me and my sleep. I even dreamed about it and after a while I found myself looking at every piece of rising ground with a view to purchasing.

We talked about money. Kate was not wealthy but between us there was no great problem regarding finance. I could sell the apartment. The city was not at that time choking in coal smog and apartments were much in demand. There would be a problem in persuading a building society to sink money in such a venture. Eventually I came back to the direct labour approach. I could be my own architect, gaffer and clerk of works, provided of course, I could get permission. In the meantime, I kept an eye out.

"What about Ruth?" I asked. "How does she take to the idea of our being married?"

"Oh, she's quite happy with the idea. When we settle down a bit she can give up boarding school, if she likes. But then I won't be at home all the time."

That was another matter I had to adjust to, the idea that she might have to travel. As yet I could not be sure how much her career meant to her and at times, I wondered if I would be marrying the whole group.

"And what about your father? Shouldn't we go and see him?"

There was a long and stony silence.

"No."

"But he is your father. I mean, isn't it time to let bygones be bygones and all that?"

"There's nothing back there for me." It was said with an air of finality, but I persisted.

"Ah, poor old Dan, living by himself all these years."

"The lads go and see him and he's not short of a few bob."

"It couldn't have been easy on him, though, in all fairness."

"Fairness? What has fairness got to do with it?" Her voice was hard.

"O.K. maybe he handled things badly at the time. He probably thought he was acting all for the best."

But she withdrew into herself and I was afraid to push any further. I should have known better than to probe an old wound.

We got married. My parents seemed quite pleased and were charmed by Kate. The not so subtle alchemy of celebrity had transformed her, I think, in their eyes from a humble caterpillar into a rather glamorous butterfly. Celebrity covers a multitude of sins. We have not as yet reached the American worship of the ideal of the self-made man. We retain still the comforting memory of when he had not a sock to his foot, but much is forgiven in the name of celebrity. Even notoriety carries a certain cachet. No amnesty was extended however, to Dan.

All in all it was a quiet affair, causing very little change in our domestic arrangements. Anto paid me the compliment of calling me a crafty bastard.

I thought of going to see Dan but put it off. When I began to feel guilty I decided again to go and again I put it off. After a while the intention became a vague aspiration, tucked safely away in the distant future, with only the dull nagging feeling that, more than likely, I would leave it too late.

Eventually I found my site, with outline planning permission for one dwelling. The old woman said she was getting out of farming. The family was all gone and her husband could no longer manage. I caught a momentary glimpse of him. He was bowed by physical labour and his hands were gnarled and distorted by arthritis. They wanted rid of the land that had nurtured, then broken them.

The site sloped towards the south, hidden from the road by a line of trees. She plodded ahead of me in her rubber boots, down a narrow muddy track and pulled back the bolt on an old wooden gate. Orange tetani spores brightened the grey crumbling wood. Bullocks regarded us curiously and edged towards us, casually eavesdropping. As Sam Goldwyn might have said, 'I didn't even ignore them'. She informed me, "You can't connect to the foul-sewer from here."

What other kind is there? I mused. She had obviously looked into things pretty thoroughly.

"Talk to the auctioneer about the details," she croaked, "but it's good enough land."

"I'm not a gardener," I replied, "'but I need enough space to make sure that nobody can build in front of me and obscure the view."

Already I was measuring the angle of the slope and projecting a horizontal from where I figured the house would be.

The view was quite spectacular, looking across the plain to the city and the mountains. On the horizon to the east ran a thin grey line of sea.

I came back at night and sat in the car looking down through the trees at the distant lights. They existed in their own right, owing nothing to thundering generators or unsightly powerlines. They had the inconsequential appeal of tinsel and Christmas-tree lights.

Kate liked the place. She liked the peace and the cold clear air. She said that she had been too long in towns and in the arid anonymity of hotels.

We bought the site and went onto bridging finance. I know a bit about bridges and I know why they call it bridging finance. The metaphor is adaptable. At Coalbrookdale there stands the first iron bridge, a cast-iron proposition. Mine was more of a suspension bridge, not a golden Gate, but more like one of those rickety liana and bamboo structures that span vertiginous chasms in the high Himalayas. Gamely I struggled across, clinging to the swaying handrails, averting my eyes from the perilous footing where one mistake might send me hurtling to certain death on the jagged rock below. My bank manager stood, scimitar in hand, threatening to sever the few remaining strands. Around me wheeled the kites that wing the midway air: registration fees, solicitors' fees, agent's fees calculated as a percentage of the gross. Figures fluttered in my head like pipistrelles aroused from their slumber.

Amazingly, my plans were passed. There was more concern expressed about the septic tank than about the dwelling itself, a lesson in getting the fundamentals right. Work began and I felt the familiar excitement at the churned-up lane, the piles of gravel and the freshly opened earth. It occupied my week-ends and the occasional mitch during the week and many hours on the telephone threatening, cajoling and pleading. There were times when I felt that maybe I should have gone for a semi-d. on some suburban estate and saved my sanity. Gradually however, it began to take shape.

We stood on the foundations and imagined the walls. We stood in the drizzle and tried to imagine the roof. The wind whistled through the openings and moaned in the sloping light shafts and we talked about glazing. Plumbers and electricians looked at each other, shrugged and went about their business and piles of timber, looking like exercises in perspective drawing, were unloaded from lorries.

When the sun shone, the light poured into the echoing shell of our house.

Twenty

I decided to go and see Dan. It was not right that there should be a breach. With a bit of luck I might stumble on a form of words that could take the bitterness out of the relationship. Whatever else he was, Dan had always been a great family man. I had in a way envied the Sheehys their unruly and happy-go-lucky household. I felt that the lads would approve of any effort in that direction. Catalyst or honest broker, either way it was worth the try.

The Sheehy lads were still a homogenous bloc to my way of thinking. They looked and talked alike and lived, in a literal and figurative way, in harmony. It was as idle a pursuit to try to separate them as it would have been to itemise the Dalton boys or the Clantons.

Their music bound them together and it was a pleasure to see how they enjoyed each other's virtuosity in performance. It would be worth a lot to draw the fabric of the family back together.

My brother, as if anticipating my thoughts, rang me. He suggested a drink at Amiens Street in the station bar. I had my first ever bottle of stout in the station bar and pretty horrible it tasted. A waste of one and a penny. A fortnight afterwards I felt the urge to have another. Of all the bars in all the world I like the station bar best, funny enough. It has less of the cosmopolitan atmosphere of an airport, but there is still the hustle and bustle of travel, the panoply of well-worn luggage and brown paper parcels. The jaded office worker has another, before hurrying to platform three or perhaps he says 'to Hell with it', and has a few more. Maybe he has missed his wonted train and it is enough to tip the balance in favour of a three day jag.

"Disposable bottles," was Anto's greeting. He regarded the offending object balefully. "All over the bloody beach. That's where they dispose of them."

I slipped onto a vacant stool beside him and ordered the same.

"You're bearing up well," he remarked. "Still living together?"

"So far so good."

"How's the house coming along?"

"Oh," I said, "pretty good. You should come out some day and have a look at it."

"We'll do that," he nodded. "Unusual by the sound of it."

"It's not my usual stock in trade, I'll admit, but we like it."

"That's the main thing. If the woman of the house doesn't like it, you can throw your hat at the whole thing."

"True enough." I wondered what he was leading up to.

"How are the folks?"

"Pretty good, by and large. Getting on I suppose."

He wiped a thin moustache of froth from his upper lip.

"And Jean and the kids?"

"Great. Not a bother."

I signalled for two more bottles. The stout had the old acrid bite that I never seemed to find anywhere but in the station bar. The taste had survived even the change over from the G.N.R.

"Your only man." Anto poured carefully. "How is Kate doing? Is she moving about much these days?"

"A bit. They're over in London for a couple of weeks. It's one aspect of the business I'm not too happy about, but it'll shake down in time. Maybe when the house is finished."

"Start a family, maybe?"

"I'd have to think about that." I laughed. "You're a bad example."

He smiled ruefully and regarded his glass.

"What about long distance tours? Would she be off to the States or Australia again?"

I looked at him curiously. "I wouldn't be too keen on that, I have to admit."

"No?"

"Well, besides the obvious, I don't mind telling you I was worried enough that time. I thought she might meet your man, Olford."

"And she didn't." He said it flatly.

"No, not a sign of him apparently. I suppose it mightn't have made any difference after all this time."

"I suppose."

"Anyway," I went on, "one good thing that came out of it all was poor old Badger's reputation. You know the way in the comics, fellas were always trying to clear somebody's name."

"Aye," he mused. "I put the story around, discreetly like, just like you told me."

"Poor ould Badger," I said. "He never had much luck."

"No, he didn't, did he? I tell you though, I feel a right fuckin' eejit, after putting your story around about your man." He looked at me with a hard, penetrating stare. "He's turned up, you know."

"Who's turned up?" I felt sweat beading my upper lip.

"John Wahab Olford."

"Jesus," I put down the glass. It beat a small tattoo on the counter as my hand shook. The nightmare was back.

"Aye, they found him in the new field where the swamp used to be. It was kind of eerie really. Hey, are you all right?" He gripped my arm. I shook my head and held onto the counter.

"I'm fine," I mumbled. "Go on."

"They're saying the ground just kind of shrank and cast him out again."

"Are they sure? I mean, they're always finding bodies in bogs and that."

"Not with the bits of a B.S.A. Gold Star tourer thrown down on top of them."

"Oh Christ!" My mind was in a turmoil. At last, he was dead. There had been times when I would have been happy to hear the news. God blast him, I thought, so he had never betrayed her at all, the bastard.

"Speaking of comics, the chap who found him said the handlebars were just sticking up out of the ground, just along the edge of the ditch, for all the world, says he, like the horns on one of Desperate Dan's cow pies." I could only manage a wan smile at the comparison.

"It's a wonder," said Anto, "he didn't turn up when they were doing the drainage. They could only have missed him by a couple of feet."

He rubbed his forehead. "I suppose that puts Badger back in the limelight for a while."

I closed my eyes and bit my lower lip.

“There’s no doubt, I suppose?” I asked, clutching at a straw.

“The plates were still on the bike.”

“Ah!”

“Yesterday morning, it seems. I heard about it when I got home last night. They took everything away for examination, including the bits of the bike.”

“What do you mean, the bits? Was it rusted away?”

“Oh yeah, but it was all cut up like, when it was being dumped. I suppose Badger was crafty enough not to leave tracks. Lookit,” he went on, “I’m sorry to tell you this. I’m sure Kate will be a bit upset. You just mind her now. I have to go.”

He took up his mackintosh and the inevitable hold-all of messages and headed for the door.

I stared straight ahead at the mirror and the spirit dispensers, optics as they are called in the trade. ‘Here’s lookin’ at you, kid’.

I felt a great pain at Kate’s absence. If only she were there. I could tell her of my fear. John Olford had come back and this time more than any other, he might steal her away from me. If only he had lived to be the rat I wanted him to be. God damn you, Badger, wherever you are, with your hands like bunches of bananas. I ordered another drink and felt a deep melancholy begin to settle on me. And, still, there was something wrong about the whole thing. *El Gavilan* had missed something.

It could have been a manifestation of a malign and embittered attitude or it could have been a reflection on the prevailing dishonesty of modern times, for Dan had acquired a doberman. A doberman couchant should be on the arms of every spare-parts and scrap dealer. It watched my tentative approach with its malevolent eyes and then advanced growling, to the furthest limit of its chain. I computed the arc of the chain and took a circuitous route towards the shed. Grass grew, luxuriantly between the car doors that leaned, clinker fashion, against the fence, wasting assets if ever I saw them.

Dan emerged from the interior gloom. He had shrunken in upon himself and looked old and tired.

“It’s yourself, isn’t it?” he greeted me, without enthusiasm and leaned against the door-jam with his hands in the pockets of his dungarees.

"That's right, Dan," I replied, extending a hand.

Dubiously he reached out and shook my hand.

"So, how are ye gettin' on?" he enquired.

"Well, you know the story, I suppose. I've been wanting to come and have a word for a good while now."

"I suppose ye have your hands full, this weather."

"Busy enough. Kate couldn't make it," I went on lamely, "she's away in London." It was as if a spasm of pain passed through him.

"Oh, a busy lady."

"She sends her regards."

"I dare say. Well, ye'd better come inside."

He opened the door to the kitchen. "I was about to make a cup o'tea."

I sat opposite him, not consciously interposing the table between us, but still keeping a wary eye on the door. I gave silent thanks that the dog was chained up. While objectively admiring my courage, I could still admit that I would rather face a murderer than a guard dog.

He put a cup of tea in front of me and we drank for a while in silence. I looked about me. It struck me that Dan probably ate on the hoof. There was no atmosphere of family about the place any more. Finally he broke the silence.

"I've been half-expectin' someone."

I steeled myself.

"How did it happen, Dan?" I waited for the outburst. It occurred to me that I should have left all the details in a sealed envelope to be opened only in the event, etc., as is the usual practice. He looked at me for what seemed a long time and picked at his front teeth with a thumbnail.

"Ah, what the hell? You might as well know."

I waited, grateful that he had not decided on violence, as yet anyway. Maybe like the cinematic villains, he would tell all before killing me. He might even tie me up first and do some gloating while I groped around for the broken bottle.

"Why did ye come to me anyway?"

"Badger never even had a decent hacksaw, had he, Dan? All he ever had was an oul' bushman with a blunt blade. All the years I worked with him he never had a decent set of tools."

Dan laughed. "That's for sure. He couldn't drive a nail in straight.

Jays, I had to keep the oul' car in runnin' order."

He drummed his fingers on the table top.

"Naw, it was my tools that we used."

"Both of you? You mean Badger was in on it too?"

"Ye might say that."

"How did it happen, Dan?" I asked again gently.

"What do ye want?" he asked with the ghost of a smile, "skin the goat?" I shrugged, not sure what he meant.

"Well, I'll tell ye. I wasn't meself them days, what with everythin'. I suppose I shouldn't've pushed her to marry Badger. She'd've done all right for herself though. He was a bit thick, I'll admit, but as decent an oul' stick as ever ye'd meet." He paused, frowning. "Naw, I suppose, lookin' back I shouldn't've pushed. I never knew about the other lad at all, at all."

He shook his head and then with sudden intensity he said, clenching his fist, "I wanted the hill, y'see. I wanted that hill. It should've been ours." I watched him without a word.

"It was ours oncet. I was always drew to it. Them people they found, they was Sheehys."

"How can you be so certain?"

"I know," he said, with finality.

"You're a shrewd man," I put in. "How come you didn't know about Kate and your man?"

"She was only a child," he said, "just a little lass." He twisted his hands together and I saw the anguish in his eyes. "Nobody ever said a father is always right. I kept it all bottled up after she told me and then one day I took a swing at him with a spanner."

"You didn't mean to kill him," I prompted. Manslaughter, though, sounds nearly worse than murder.

"I would have, but Badger got between us."

"I don't quite follow."

"It was down in the field below the wood. Badger was tryin' to get the trailer off the draw-bar of the tractor. He wanted to get the chain harrow on. The bloody thing was jammed an' he came up here for a lend of a spanner."

"So you went with him?"

"Aye. I took the big monkey wrench. I was glad of somethin' to do. When we got back your man was there waitin'. He wanted to talk to

Badger. Wanted to sort things out, he said. Do the decent thing, he said. The decent thing, how are ye!"

"So you took a swing?"

He made a futile sort of gesture with one hand. "I suppose I saw red. She was me own little lass. I never laid a hand on a body in anger in all me life. Ah Jays." His eyes filled up and he rubbed at his nose. "Badger steps in and sends him flying outa the ways and grabs me by the wrist. Nearly took the arm off me."

"But who killed him?"

"He fell back again' the tailboard o'the trailer and one o'the harrow pins went into the back of his head. He sort of hung there lookin' at the two of us. Jays, I can still see him." His eyes stared, unfocussed.

"It was an accident. Why didn't you report it?"

"Who'd've believed us?" He shrugged. "Anyway ye could hardly call it an accident, now, could ye?"

"And then?"

"We put him in the trailer with the bike and thrun a few sacks over him. I got me hacksaws. It was Badger's idea. He said we could still carry on like before. We carried the bits out into the swamp. No tracks like, ye know."

"What else did Badger say?"

"What did he say? He said he couldn't've done that to a Norton." Despite myself I had to smile. "No I suppose he couldn't."

"Badger said if we kep' quiet it would all blow over."

"He miscalculated though, didn't he?"

"He never gave a damn about all that. It was Kate he wanted. He'd have gev anythin' for that girl."

That I could understand.

"It's funny, but I'm glad I told someone at last. I'm even glad the hill is gone. It never had luck. What will ye do now?"

"I don't know," I said. "Talk to Kate, maybe." I shrugged. "She's bound to hear something."

"Are ye good to her?" he asked after a while.

"Try to be," I said.

"Aye. Ye know, I always liked that young lad, young Olford. That's the funny part."

I could see very little humour in anything just then. My brilliant powers of detection had solved the case only to leave the sleuth without a clue as to what to do next. The hound of the Baskervilles eyed me balefully as I made my way out and then turned away in contempt.

The London trip had been very successful. Recording had gone well. There had been concerts. I felt the same stab of irritation that I always felt when I thought of how she could command an audience. I could never understand why an audience was so important. It was enough for me that they enjoyed each other's music. Why then try to win over an audience? I felt no envy of her undoubted appeal to her listeners. I kept aloof from the business. That particular Kate was for public consumption.

I broke the news as gently as I could on the way back from the airport. We walked through the park and sat on a bench. The air was frosty and the trees were bare. She turned her coat collar up and scuffled the gravel with her heels.

"It was an accident," I said, alarmed by her silence.

She made no reply.

"For what it's worth, he never ran out on you." I had not wanted to say it, but I thought it might make it a bit easier for her. Deep down, I thought it might be no harm to notch up a charitable remark, a credit to set against the black bile that had welled up whenever I heard his name. I felt like a hypocrite.

Kate nodded silently, shoving her hands into her pockets. She put me in mind of a child who has had a bad fall and is still too shocked to cry. I put my arm around her and felt the tension in her.

"Tell me the whole story," she said after a while. "You went to see my father didn't you?"

"I did, yes."

"I had a feeling you would."

I told her Dan's story, going easy on the gruesome details. "It was an accident," I said again. I had made some discreet enquiries, of a hypothetical nature, as one might enquire about a shameful disease. Opinions varied from conspiracy to murder, through manslaughter to death by misadventure. I inclined towards the third option myself, but Dan had taken the first swing.

"Have you told anyone about this?" she asked at last.

"No. I'm not the prosecutor." I wondered if I had now become an accessory after the fact. Badger at least would be in the clear but

Badger was dead. It could only make trouble for Dan. Perhaps that is too pragmatic an approach for the legal mind, although it has its merits. I wished that she would say something, but she just gazed into vacuity.

"We should go indoors," I suggested. "You look exhausted."

"In a while," she murmured. "In a little while."

I stood up. Movement is good therapy. "It's getting very cold."

"Go on," she said, "I want to be by myself for a little while."

I went indoors. Food, I decided, restores the flagging spirits. It is probably gross to suggest that food is one of the great pleasures of being alive and a sure antidote to thoughts of death. The smell of cooking would take her mind off things. In some areas I admit, I am not the most sensitive.

I waited. The soup cooled. Tectonic plates formed on the surface. I paced about and looked out the window at the dusk. Fog lurked under the trees. There was no sign of her in the park. Lights came on in the convent opposite. Soon it was dark. I looked at the soup. It had gone cold and had begun to separate into its components. Drops of condensation from the saucepan lid had pockmarked the surface. It looked like a repulsive slime. I swilled it down the sink.

I watched the news and drank coffee, waiting for the sound of a footstep and the comforting grate of her key. I went outside and stood at the door willing her to appear. No familiar shape loomed out of the streetlight. The stars were bright, like pyrites in the inky blackness. I wandered around. The park was padlocked. Panic rose inside me. I saw her walking alone in some darkened street, stalked by amorphous figures that slunk away from the pools of dim yellow light.

I drove around the area with lights full on and when I returned her car was gone. It was some relief to know that she was still alive but I feared for her, driving in a disturbed state of mind. I could feel her pain and I was helpless to do anything. I rang her brothers but she had not been in touch. I rang Ruth's school ostensibly to let her know that her mother was home. She had heard nothing. I baulked at calling the police. I imagined their bemused looks as I explained that my wife had been missing for several hours, that she had gone out for a drive. No, there had been no row. Yes, perhaps I should go home and wait to see if she phoned. Very likely she would be home before long. I could of course, mention that her father had killed her lover, the father of her child and that the body had been hidden for many years only to pop up out of the ground a few days before. That should get me some attention. It might even bring the sergeant to the desk, but I had no desire to draw that much attention on myself. I dislike performing in front of an audience.

I waited up all night dozing fitfully. It is true that the spirits are at their lowest ebb in the small hours. The night seemed interminable and I woke with a stiff neck. I wandered from room to room and stood for a long time at the window. There was a spectacular sunrise. A coven of rooks skulked in a high tree that swayed in the wind. It was mid-winter.

The day dragged on. I ate some food of the consistency of newspaper. I looked at sheaves of plans and half finished work and I made some phone calls. The day dragged into afternoon and the light failed. Surely she would come. I heard childrens' voices and the hum of traffic and I moved things around on my desk.

I went out again towards evening but hurried back in order to be there.

I looked at the hollow-eyed, unshaven stranger in the mirror and I washed my teeth. For a long time I sat listening and at some point I knew that she would not be coming back that night. I lay back on the couch in dumb misery and slipped into a fitful sleep.

John Olford spoke to me. He looked well, but much younger than I expected.

"Well, John," I said amiably, "how are things?"

"Ah," he said, "d'you know, I'd love a spin on that old bike of mine."

"The Gold Star? A great bike." I could afford to be magnanimous towards the boy.

"No. My first one. The old *Excelsior*." He laughed. "You never get over your first love."

"Indeed you don't," I agreed and opened my eyes.

In the bleary light a silver fish glided across the floor. I watched his dull pewter sheen. What did he think of it all? There was an old woman in the hospital, Kate told me, who used to chase the cockroaches with the lavatory brush. "Get back in the wall," she used to say. "Get back in the wall, or they'll kill ye. There's life in them things." She was completely mad of course. The silverfish flickered and disappeared.

I was cold and cramped. The central heating had not come on. The old people used to warn against central heating. 'You'll be crucified with colds. The germs love a warm atmosphere'. A Spartan life may be devoid of comfort, but by God, you'll be healthy. I hold no loyalty towards freezing lino. Germs have rights too, I suppose.

The sun struggled upwards through an armada of grey, sluggish cumulus clouds. The sky looked like a photograph of the Normandy landings. High above the cumulus were white wisps of cirrus, already taking on a pink tinge from the labouring sun. A red sky in the morning.

I drove through the still silent city, out to the sea at the Bull where the Corporation had put in a new causeway, effectively killing the lagoon. The rushes and grass were withered and sere, Solzhenitsyn country, the monotony relieved by a rusty tar barrel. I regretted not having tucked a lump of black bread under my armpit. The chimneys of the power station across the bay sent up their frivolous white plumes with a certain panache.

Movement was the best thing. I decided to go out to the house. In fact there were a few things to be checked. It was something to do. I felt a vague stirring of anger. She was playing to the gallery again, some invisible gallery in her own mind, like the madman in the story who sat applauding in the empty theatre, at once both entertainer and audience. I could always stand back and admire her performance without succumbing to it.

The men were already on the site, I was pleased to note. They were keen to get the main work finished before Christmas. I knew that they had a few jobs lined up and had already marked their territory with a load of gravel and a few blocks, to warn off other tenders.

I walked around. The windows were glazed, double-glazed in fact, another concession to the degeneracy of the race. Floorboards were down and there was the exciting smell of sawn timber in the air. A fireplace of soft coloured Leitrim limestone was in place.

"A great draw on that chimney," the builder assured me.

We walked up over the roof. Sheets of interlocking foam insulation gave it an igloo appearance.

"We'll get the aggregate over that today," he assured me and went about his business.

I looked down the hill and across the plain towards the mountains. The wind coming out of the north east cut through my clothes, chilling me through. I went down again and stood inside looking at the landscape. I thought I saw a fleck of snow. And another one.

The house had become a matter of purely technical interest. I could probably find a buyer. There had to be at least one eccentric with a few bob in his pocket. I watched a black speck above the trees, a kestrel. Yes. It stopped and hung quivering in the air, a windhover. Romulus had sited his city by following the flight of eagles. A good omen. And then he killed his brother.

I looked down at the landscape and thought of the generations that had held it and lost it since time began. Like the silverfish, they thought that their concerns were important. The kestrel dropped behind the black winter hedgerows. Snow was falling.

"I might leave it," said the builder's voice behind me.

"What?" I had forgotten about him.

"The aggregate. There's a bit of an oul' leak gettin' in. Just a tiny patch of damp. Mightn't be anything to worry about, but I better have a look at it."

It looked about the size of a half crown.

"If it got in at the oul' steel you might have a problem in a few years."

"What do you think?"

He rubbed his nose with the knuckle of his forefinger and frowned.

"Maybe the oul' insulation will keep it out. I dunno."

We looked up at the offending stain.

"Leave it," said Kate's voice behind us. "It will be all right."

She was smiling as she took my hand.

"Leave it," I agreed. "We wouldn't want to offend the gentry."

The builder looked at us with incomprehension. He took off his hat and scratched his temple.

"If you want my opinion the whole thing has to come off again."

"It's fine," I said. "Don't worry about it." We were laughing, but not at him. He shrugged. "On your own heads be it." He went away shaking his head.

She sat on the carpenter's stool. It was criss-crossed with mitre cuts and hacked along the edge. Splinters tugged at the threads of her coat. I asked no questions. She held her hands in her lap.

"Did you see the kestrel?" she asked.

"Yes. I was watching him and thinking about us, as a matter of fact."

"I went to see me Da."

For an instant she was ten years old. I felt a constriction in my throat and could say nothing.

"He went in and made a statement."

"Ah!"

"There might be charges. I don't know."

"I'm glad you went."

She put her head to one side and looked at me. "Then I came home."

While we had been talking the world outside had turned white. Snow whirled out of the grey overcast. Soft plumes drifted down the glass. She came and stood beside me and I drew her close. The world looked like a clean fresh page.